Brandon has all the problems eighteen-year-old guys have — an overbearing mother, a little brother he could do without, and two slightly pushy best friends. When he goes dancing one night, he doesn't expect to find himself with more problems — and a mate.

Maddox is a loner, and he likes it. He trusts his numerous pets more than most humans, but some people don't allow him to push them away, like Asher, his coworker and best friend. Asher is the only reason Maddox finds himself dragged to the club even though he hates crowds and dancing. And when he steps into the bathroom and realizes something is happening in one of the stalls, the evening takes a turn for the worse. Someone drugged his mate and assaulted him.

Brandon knows he was lucky Maddox stepped in when he did, but when the man who drugged him escapes before being taken to the council jail, he expects things to go south. He's not sure why Maddox offers him to stay at his house, since he clearly loves living alone, but he's not about to say no to the possibility of getting to know his mate better, even though Maddox keeps him at arm's length.

But the man who drugged Brandon is on the run, and he's coming for Brandon. Will Maddox be able to keep his mate safe — even from himself? Or will he break Brandon's heart before losing him?

Brandon
Copyright © 2019 Catherine Lievens
ISBN: 978-1-4874-2415-2
Cover art by Angela Waters

Published by eXtasy Books Inc or
Devine Destinies, an imprint of eXtasy Books Inc

Look for us online at:
www.eXtasybooks.com or www.devinedestinies.com

Brandon
Wyoming Shifters: 12 Years Later Book 7

By

Catherine Lievens

CHAPTER ONE

"Brandon?"

Brandon groaned and wondered if his mom was going to check his bedroom. Probably. Should he hide in the closet? He was tempted to do that, but he knew better. His mom knew he was home, so she'd check the bathroom at the very least, and if she didn't find him, she'd freak out. She'd been crazy protective since that thing with Brandon's dad had happened, and he wanted to hide from her, not scare her to death.

He sighed. "I'm in my bedroom!" he called back. He hoped she wouldn't want to talk again. They'd already done this a few times, and it became more uncomfortable with every conversation.

His bedroom door opened. He put down his phone and watched his mother walk in with an armful of folded laundry. "You know you don't have to bring it to me," he said, even though he knew it was a lost cause. It used to be that he and Jason had to go to the laundry room to get their clean clothes and put them away, which was okay with Brandon. But now their mom had started doing everything in the house as if she was afraid they might break if they had to put laundry away. It was ridiculous, but no matter how many times Brandon told her to stop, she didn't.

She smiled. "I know, but I was looking for you anyway." She put it on the dresser and reached for the top drawer, but that was too much for Brandon.

He hopped up from his bed. "That's fine, Mom. I'll do it

myself. Thanks for bringing it here, though."

She froze. "Are you sure?"

"Yes." Brandon thought she was probably bored or something like that. He wanted to suggest she find something to do, like a job or whatever, but he knew better. She'd get offended.

She leaned back against the dresser. "So, what are you up to?"

"Nothing much. I was texting Lee. We're going to the fire pit later."

"What about now? Are you busy?"

There she went. "Not really."

"Your homework?"

"Is done. I just have to finish reading some stuff, but I have time."

"Good. How are you, Brandon?"

Brandon sighed. "I'm fine, Mom."

"Are you sure? What happened with your dad was—"

"Had been happening for a while, so it wasn't a surprise."

"You couldn't have known your father was gay."

"I didn't, but once you told us you were getting divorced, well, it made me think and realize something had been wrong all along. Come on, Mom. We've already talked about this."

"I know but having already talked about it doesn't mean we shouldn't do it again. I'm sure you have questions, or that you're worried about things."

"I'm not. I swear I'm not. I know you and Dad still love Jason and me. I know you're both happier this way." Although Brandon wasn't too sure his mother was. She'd told him and Jason this was the right thing to do because she and their dad had never been in love and they both deserved a real relationship, but while Brandon's dad had bonded with his mate and was happy, his mom seemed lost these days.

Brandon hated it, and he hated that she'd turned all her attention on him and Jason. He felt like she was always hovering, always watching him and just being there even when he'd rather be alone. He loved her, but it was getting to be too much, and he wished he could be free for a bit.

Brandon loved his mom, but she'd gone from being a normal mom to always being around asking questions, and *that*, he didn't like.

He cleared his throat. "Look, I'm okay. I promise. I'm glad you and Dad decided to do what you thought was best and that you're both happier now." And that he wouldn't have to marry some random girl his grandfather had picked for him, but he didn't say that. His mom would go on her usual rant about it, and he'd heard it often enough.

She hesitated. "Just . . . you know you can come to me for anything, right? I won't judge you."

"I know." But still, he hadn't yet told her he was gay. His dad knew because they'd talked about it when they'd had the conversation about Matt and his father bonding, but he was afraid to tell his mom. He knew she wouldn't care, but he didn't want to hurt her. Whatever she said, however well she hid it, it was impossible that she hadn't been hurt by Brandon's dad bonding with Matt, and Brandon didn't want to make things worse for her. Besides, he'd been hiding it for years. Waiting a few more months wouldn't hurt him, not when he already knew she wouldn't care.

He grabbed his phone from the bed. "I need to go."

"Oh?"

"I told you, Lee and I were going to meet at the fire pit."

"I thought you said that was later, though."

It was supposed to be, but Brandon was *not* going to hang around the house when his mom wanted to talk about his feelings. "Yeah, but he told me he doesn't have anything to do right now, so we're going to meet sooner."

"Oh. Will you be back for dinner?"

"I don't know, Mom. I'll let you know, okay?"

Brandon left the house in a hurry, only stopping to grab his wallet and a jacket. He breathed easier once he was in the forest. He was worried about his mom, but he wished she wouldn't pour all the love she had on him and Jason. She needed someone in her life now that Brandon's dad wasn't in the picture for her anymore, but Brandon wasn't sure how to make that happen. Besides, the thought of his mother with someone who wasn't his dad was still weird, maybe because she was still alone. It was easier to imagine his dad with someone else, since he had Matt and they were both a part of Brandon's life.

He got to the fire pit and flopped onto one of the benches there, folding his leg under himself. He needed to find a way to get his mom to stop asking him if he was okay. He'd tried telling her more than once, but then she just asked him about his life, what he did with his friends, if he had a girlfriend — things he didn't want to talk to her about.

"You're pouting again," Lee said as he sat next to Brandon on the bench.

"It's my mom."

Lee grimaced and pushed his fringe away from his forehead. "What did she do now?"

"The usual. She's worried I didn't take the divorce well."

"Still? I thought you told her you're okay with it."

"I did. Lots of times."

"So what are you gonna do?"

Brandon sighed. "I don't know."

"What about moving in with your dad? He's better, right? Or are you weirded out by the fact that he's mated to a guy?"

"Nah. I like Matt, and my dad's happier than he's ever been."

"Then go."

It was something Brandon had already thought about, of course, but could he really leave his mom? "I don't know."

Lee leaned closer. "I mean, your parents both have a room for you. They said you could stay with who you wanted, right?"

"Yeah." But Brandon knew his mom would rather have him live with her at home.

"Besides, you're going to move soon anyway. High school's almost over. Or did you change your mind about us living together?"

"Don't say stupid things." But Brandon hadn't told his parents he and Lee had been planning to move in together after school. Neither of them knew if they wanted to go to college, even though they'd applied. But they did know they wanted out of their parents' houses. "Maybe I should stay with her until then."

"Or maybe you should live with your dad. If staying with your mom really makes you uncomfortable . . ."

It did. Brandon had always been closer to his father than to his mother, while Jason was the opposite, especially since the divorce. "I don't want to hurt her."

"I get that, but you're going to have to leave soon anyway. The way I see it, she's trying to tie you to her."

"She wouldn't do that."

"Maybe not consciously, no. But you're staying because you don't want her to be hurt, right? Not because you want to. Because of her. And she just lost her husband completely. They didn't just divorce. Your dad met his mate."

"They weren't in love."

"Maybe not, but they were together for a long time. It has to be hard to lose someone that important."

Brandon wrinkled his nose. "How do you even know that?"

Lee shrugged. "I have eyes."

And he knew how to use them. Lee had always been an observer, ever since he'd moved in with the pack as a kid. They never talked about his past, but Brandon knew it wasn't a nice one.

Thinking about it made Brandon realize he was lucky. He had both his parents, and they both loved him. Still, he was going to have to talk to his father and see if he'd allow him to move in with him and Matt.

Maddox rubbed the top of the Beagle's head and gently pushed him away. He snuck out of the cage and locked it, doing his best to ignore the dog's whining. God, he wished he could take all of them home. And he did his best to, but his place was already nearing full capacity. He'd taken yet another cat home two weeks ago. Queen Elizabeth was doing great, although she was still wary of Maddox's dogs.

Maddox walked back to the break room, needing some time. He loved his job at the shelter, but sometimes it hurt. He wanted to be able to do more, to find all the dogs and cats a loving home. But even when he and the others managed to empty some of the cages, new occupants arrived. It was a cycle that never ended.

Asher was in the break room when Maddox got there, eating yogurt and smiling at his phone. Maddox knew Asher's mate was always involved when he was smiling that way, so he was probably texting Terry.

He looked up when he heard Maddox, though, and pushed his phone away. "Hey. I thought you'd never take your break."

"I was with the dogs."

Asher grimaced. "Which one are you taking home today?"

Maddox rolled his eyes. He would have been offended if Asher hadn't been wrong about his habit. "None of them." Not tonight anyway. Maybe. "Queen Elizabeth still isn't used to the ones at home. I don't want to fuck it up by adding a new one."

"I don't know how you come up with those names."

Maddox sat in the chair opposite Asher. "I just watch the animals."

"Someday you're going to have so many of them you'll find yourself out of a bed. How many sleep with you?"

"That's what I have a king size bed for, Ash. It's not like I share it with anyone."

"Why not? What about a boyfriend?"

Maddox shrugged. He wasn't going to talk about that. He never did, not even with Asher, even though they were friends and co-workers. "You know there's no one."

"For now. You're going to find someone sooner or later."

"Maybe." Maddox wasn't counting on that, though. He was fine on his own. He liked being on his own, with his dogs and his cats and the rest of the small menagerie he had.

"*Maybe*, Maddox? Come on. You're grumpy and everything, but that doesn't mean you have to spend the rest of your life alone."

"Who said anything about the rest of my life? Besides, I'm not alone. I have you and my family."

"Well, yeah, but it's not the same. I have you and my family, too, but Terry's different."

"How about this? I'll welcome my mate when I find him, but in the meantime, you won't push for me to look for a boyfriend or whatever you're thinking of."

Asher scowled and waved his spoon at Maddox. "You know that's not fair. You might never find your mate."

"But I might also meet him tomorrow, right?"

"Still. Are you saying you'll stay alone if you don't? He

doesn't *have* to be your mate. You could be happy with someone else. You could fall in love even without a bond."

But then the man he fell for wouldn't have anything keeping him with Maddox. The man could leave Maddox or kick him out like his parents had. He'd been lucky, because he'd found a new family with the pack, but a boyfriend? No. He had enough friends who'd been dumped to know he was better off without one. "I won't."

Asher blinked. "You won't what? Fall in love?"

Maddox winced. He hadn't meant to say that out loud. He did that sometimes. He had the tendency to talk to his animals, and they didn't answer or repeat what he told them, so he didn't use his brain-to-mouth filter with them. He had to with Asher and their friends, though. "I meant that I don't want to fall in love right now. I have plenty of stuff in my life right now. I wouldn't have the time for a boyfriend."

"But you would for your mate? If you met him, that is."

"I would make time for him." Maybe. If he liked animals and if he didn't care that Maddox had so many, and that he enjoyed being alone more than being with other people.

"Then surely you can make time for a boyfriend, or at least to meet new people."

"Can we not talk about this? If you remember, I never asked you about Terry or why the two of you weren't together even though I knew you were mates."

Asher grimaced. "True. Sorry. I'm just worried. I guess I want everyone to be as happy as I am, especially you. I know you like being alone, and I get it, but still. You're human, and you need human interaction."

Maddox leaned over the table and smacked a kiss on the tip of Asher's nose. "I know you're doing this because you care, and I'm grateful to have you in my life. It would be easier for you to ignore me and stop worrying. I know I'm not an easy person to deal with even on my best days. But I'm fine, Asher. I swear. I have everything I want in life."

"Except a boyfriend."

Maddox shrugged. "Who said I wanted one. I told you, I'm fine on my own. No one to care if I take home another cat, no one to bug me about where I was and with whom." And no one to leave him when they'd had enough. Maddox wouldn't get kicked out again since he owned his house in pack territory, but he could be left, and he wasn't going to risk it. With the way he still hurt over his parents' rejection, he couldn't imagine how much it would hurt from someone he allowed himself to fall in love with.

Asher sniffed. "All right, I'll stop bugging you on this, but you have to promise me something."

Maddox rolled his eyes. "What?"

"If you do meet someone, you're going to give him a chance."

Maddox didn't want to make a promise he wouldn't keep. "If I meet my mate, I'll give him a chance." After all, there would be a bond between them that would make it next to impossible for his mate to leave him, especially if they bonded. Maddox could deal with that, or at least he hoped so.

Asher's eyes narrowed. "That's not what I said."

"I know, but you won't get anything else from me. Come on, Ash. I'm happy even though I don't have a man. Not everyone needs love."

Asher's smile was soft and sad. "Yeah, we do."

"Okay, then not everyone needs that kind of love. I have you and the others, and my family. I have enough love in my life."

"I'd believe that if you didn't spend your time avoiding me and everyone else, but okay."

Maddox was glad when Asher started talking about Terry. He didn't particularly care for Asher's mate, but Asher was one of his best friends, and no matter how little Maddox thought of the guy—how could he not have realized he and Asher were mates—nothing would change that fact. Besides, Asher was happy now, and that was all that mattered.

Asher's steady conversation meant Maddox could tune out for a bit. If he was honest with himself, he wouldn't mind having someone human to go home to. He loved his animals, but they weren't the best conversationalists, and sometimes, that was what Maddox wanted. He could pick up the phone and call his friends or his family, but everyone had their own lives and their mates or significant other. He had his dogs and his cats, and they were great for cuddling, but they were furry, and not of the sexy kind.

Maddox sighed. Yeah, he wanted someone in his life, but not enough to risk being left. He'd already gone through that, and the longing for human company didn't even come close to the pain of losing someone he loved. He'd be fine with his animals. He always had been.

Love was for people who could put themselves out there and take a risk, but Maddox's heart was already bruised and battered. It wouldn't stand another beating, and he wasn't going to risk having it broken.

Brandon knocked once before pushing the front door open. He stepped into his dad's house and called out, "Dad?"

"In the kitchen!" Brandon's dad called back.

Brandon smiled and toed his shoes off. He left them by the door and padded to the kitchen, smiling when he found his dad sitting at the table sipping coffee. "Hey."

His dad looked up. "Brandon. I didn't expect you today."

Brandon shrugged and sat in front of his dad. "I wasn't planning to come by."

"What changed your mind?"

Brandon hesitated. He was going to have to explain why he was there, but should he wait? "I need to talk to you."

Brandon's dad frowned and put down his cup, but before he could say anything, the back door opened and Matt came in. He paused when he saw Brandon, but only for a moment. Brandon knew Matt still felt awkward about dealing with him and Jason, and he understood. Hell, he was awkward too. He was happy for his dad, and he could see how much Matt meant to him, but that didn't mean everything was perfect now, especially not when they were still all trying to fit into each other's life.

But the look on Brandon's dad's face when he saw Matt was worth every minute of discomfort. He never used to smile that way, not when he'd still been married to Brandon's mom. Brandon supposed some people would think he was weird because he didn't have a problem with the divorce or his dad mating a guy, but he honestly didn't care. He'd be a hypocrite, considering he was gay, and he'd seen first-hand how unhappy his parents had both been, but especially his dad.

He wasn't anymore.

"I can come back later," Matt said, looking at Brandon.

Brandon smiled at him. "You don't have to. I mean, you're Dad's mate, so you're going to find out sooner rather than later. Besides, this has to do with you as much as with Dad, so . . ." Brandon shrugged. "You might as well stay."

"Are you sure?"

"Yes. Come on, sit with us."

Brandon knew he'd done the right thing, but that impression strengthened when his dad took Matt's hand once he was sitting at the table with them. He squeezed it, and they exchanged a glance that told Brandon how much they loved each other. He'd never seen that kind of stuff between his parents.

Then Matt's cheeks flushed and he cleared his throat—he must have realized Brandon was watching them.

Brandon grinned at him. "I know you don't need my approval or whatever, but you two are perfect for each other."

The red on Matt's cheeks deepened. "Uh, thank you?"

"Are you two finished with the love fest?" Brandon's dad asked. He was smiling, and Brandon smiled back.

He loved his mom, but he already felt more relaxed than he ever did with her. He knew his dad wouldn't push for answers or to talk about whatever was on Brandon's mind. He was giving Brandon time to work things out, and Brandon was glad.

He wasn't sure how to broach the subject, though, no matter how long he thought about it. "Hey, you remember when you told me I could stay here however long I wanted whenever I wanted?" he asked his dad.

His dad frowned. "Of course I do. Why? Do to want to spend the night? You don't have to ask, Brandon. This is your house as much as it is Jason's and ours."

Brandon rubbed his palms on his thighs. "I know that. But I meant staying here full time, not only for the night."

The frown in his dad's face deepened. "Did something happen with your mother?"

"Not really. I *can* stay here with you, though, right?"

"Of course you can. What does your mother think about this, though?"

Brandon grimaced. "I haven't told her yet. I wanted to be sure it was okay with you first. Well, with you and Matt, of course." Because there was no way Brandon would stay here if Matt didn't want him to. He wanted his dad to be happy, and that wouldn't happen if he and Matt fought because of him. He could stay with his mom until he finished high school. He would probably go crazy over her hovering, but he could do it.

"As Colin said, this is your home, too, Brandon. You're welcome to stay here with us for as long as you need," Matt said.

"Are you sure? I'd understand if you'd rather have my dad all to yourself."

Matt's cheeks went red again. "I won't deny I'm not used to sharing a house with you and that we'll probably have to set some ground rules and, well, get used to each other, but that doesn't mean I won't let you stay here. You're Colin's son. You're part of the package I accepted when I decided to bond with him. So neither of you should worry about me. I'm one hundred percent okay with you and your brother staying here or even moving in."

"Is Jason moving in, too?" Brandon's dad asked.

"I don't think so. I haven't talked to him, though." That wasn't anything new. Brandon and Jason weren't that close.

"Why do you want to move, Brandon?"

Brandon sighed. "I know Mom loves me, but she always wants to talk about what happened. She's always around, asking me how am I, if I'm okay with you and Matt, things like that. And no matter how many times I tell her I am, it's like she doesn't believe me, so she keeps pushing." Brandon bit his lower lip. "I haven't even told her I'm gay yet."

"Why not? You know she won't care. She loves you the way you are."

"I know, but I don't want to hurt her."

Brandon's dad leaned back in his chair. "You mean like I did?"

Shit. "That's not what I said."

"But it's what happened."

"Come on, Dad. We both know you're not the bad guy here. There are no bad guys in this situation." Except for Brandon's grandfather, but his dad had dealt with him.

Brandon was relieved he wouldn't have to marry whatever girl his grandfather had chosen for him. He could only imagine how his father had felt when he'd been forced to marry Brandon's mom.

He had conflicting feelings about that, but the main one was that even though his dad had been hurt for a long time, Brandon it was the result, and he was happy to be alive. But him being alive meant his dad had been unhappy for twenty years, which was why Brandon was conflicted.

"So the reason you want to move in with us is that you're uncomfortable with your mother?"

"Kinda? I mean, yeah, mostly. I just wish she didn't always ask me how I am and stuff, you know? But really, things haven't been the same since you left. I love both of you, but you know I've always been closer to you."

Brandon's dad smiled. "And Jason has always been closer to her."

"Yeah, exactly. I know I could just get a place of my own, or with Lee, but I don't want to live on my own just yet."

"You shouldn't. You're not even out of high school yet."

"So, can I stay here? I know it's going to cause problems with Mom. I wish it didn't, but I've thought about it, and I wouldn't ask if I wasn't sure this is what I want."

His dad sighed. "I know. And yes, it's going to cause problems. She's been especially protective of you and your brother since the divorce. But if you really feel more comfortable here, then I'll talk to her."

Brandon wanted to let his dad do the talking. His dad wouldn't mind. But Brandon knew he needed to be the one to talk to his mom. *He* was moving out, not his dad. "I'll talk to her, Dad."

"How about we do it together? You can tell her you want to move in with me, and I'll tell her it's fine and that, of course, she's welcome to come by any time she wants to check on you."

Matt cleared his throat. "Any time?"

Brandon's dad smiled. "Within reason, of course. Don't worry. I'll make sure she doesn't come every day. I know she'll be worried about Brandon, but I've been a father for as long as she's been a mother. I can take care of our sons as well as she can."

For some reason, Brandon doubted that would change his mom's mind.

Maddox crouched in front of the cage and silently opened it. The Beagle inside looked at him with his big eyes—eyes Maddox couldn't say no to. "Come on, Colonel Bau. Let's get you out of here."

He wiggled his fingers, and the dog moved toward him. They were already friends, since Maddox had been taking care of him since he'd arrived at the shelter. He trusted Maddox, and Maddox laughed when he licked his face. "Good boy. Come on. I'm taking you home." And so what if that meant Asher was right and that Maddox had more animal friends than human ones? Colonel Bau needed him, and he needed the unconditional love his furry friends gave him. At least they would never kick him out or abandon him. Besides, he only had two dogs. He could take in a third, especially when he was as cute as Colonel Bau.

Maddox had already filled in and signed all the forms for the adoption, so he hooked the leash onto Colonel Bau's collar and led him to the exit. He'd waited until everyone else was gone so Asher wouldn't bug him about taking in another dog, so he made a quick exit, hauling Colonel Bau into his truck and driving toward home. He relaxed as he did so, happy to be going home, and to have another dog. He loved animals, and he'd seen enough of Colonel Bau to know he loved him back. The poor dog didn't deserve to spend the rest of his life in the shelter, and since he was an older dog, people weren't fighting to adopt him.

Well, that wasn't a problem now. Maddox had adopted him, and when he took in an animal, it was for life. Colonel Bau was set.

The dog was slightly wary when Maddox led him into his new home, probably a mix of being in a new place and the smells and sounds of the other animals living there. Maddox left the Beagle in his living room and went to free his other two dogs — Madame Mimsy and Princess Pawpington — from their crates. They ran around his ankles as Queen Elizabeth watched them from her spot on the kitchen counter. She was a fluffy, haughty cat, and she didn't like being cuddled, although she sometimes made an exception for Maddox.

"All right, all right. Give me the time to take everything out, and I'll feed you, loves," Maddox told the animals as he moved around the kitchen.

That seemed to be the magic word. Colonel Bau appeared at the kitchen door, followed by Lord Nibbles and King McFluff, two of Maddox's cats. The last one, Prince Whiskerton, was always late, so Maddox wasn't worried that he wasn't here yet.

He busied himself with the food, dishing it and putting down all the bowls in his usual order — first the cats because they wouldn't listen to him when he told them to stay, then the dogs, who usually obeyed him. Colonel Bau got his own bowl — Maddox always had a few of those around, just in case.

Once that was done, he fed his parrot, Fitz, then brought carrots and lettuce out to his two rabbits, Bugs and Bunny. Once that was done, it was time for Maddox to take care of himself. He stuck some leftovers in the microwave and headed for the bathroom as they heated, but he stopped when he heard the sound of tires on the gravel outside his house. He didn't often get visitors, and even when he did, it wasn't late at night. Of course, it was late only for him, since his friends didn't think anything of going out at ten PM, but he had to work tomorrow, and he still had to shower and eat. It was already eight-thirty PM, so he wouldn't have a lot of time to relax and read, especially not with Colonel Bau being new.

Maddox could hear voices and footsteps. He sighed when he recognized one of the voices as Asher's and walked to the front door before he could knock. He opened it, and sure enough, Asher's fist was raised. He almost knocked on Maddox's nose, chuckling when he noticed the open door. "Oops. Hey, Maddox."

Asher wasn't alone. Terry was with him—of course he was, when did those two ever do something without the other—as well as Gabriel and Alice. Maddox was friends with all of them, but that didn't mean he was happy to see them. He liked his friends in small doses, which meant not all together. "This looks like an intervention." He wouldn't be surprised if it was, not after the conversation he'd had with Asher.

Asher grimaced. "It kind of is, I mean, it's not an intervention per se, but everyone was worried about you, so we decided to come around and see if we could drag you out or something."

Alice pushed past Maddox, ignoring his scowl. "We're taking you to the club to dance. I'm picking your clothes. Do you have anything that's not covered in animal hair?"

"I didn't invite you to come in," he yelled after her, but she ignored him.

He wasn't surprised. He turned his attention back to Asher and gave him his best glare. "I don't want to go dancing. I hate dancing and clubs."

"Maybe, but it will do you good to come. You spend too much time with your cats." He cocked his head and looked at something behind Maddox. "And your dogs. All *three* of them."

Maddox didn't blush. *Nope.* "What?"

"I see Colonel Bau has a new home."

"He was lonely at the shelter."

"Well, he sure won't be here. I think Prince Whiskerton likes him."

Terry made a strangled sound. Maddox glared at him, too, even though he was probably the only one who couldn't have cared less if Maddox went dancing with their little group. He was Asher's mate, but that didn't mean he and Maddox were friends. "What?" Maddox snapped.

Terry shook his head. "Nothing. I mean... Prince Whiskerton?"

"I don't think the way I name my pets is any of your business."

Asher grinned and turned to look at his mate. "Wait until you meet Princess Pawpington and Lord Nibbles."

That did it. Terry giggled, then pressed his lips together, but Maddox could see he was about to explode. He rolled his eyes and stepped aside to let the buggers in. He scowled at Gabriel, too, even though the poor guy hadn't said anything and was probably there because Alice had dragged him along. They were kindred spirits, happier with staying home than going out but going anyway to make their friends happy.

Pity they weren't all of the furry kind, because Maddox had no problem dealing with those.

He left the three in his living room fawning over his pets and went to his bedroom. He grimaced when he saw the result of Alice's nosiness. Half of his wardrobe was on the bed, the other half precariously hanging from Alice's arm as she examined every single piece of clothing before dumping it with the rest.

She looked up when Maddox came in. "Mad, do you *really* not have anything nice looking?"

Maddox looked down at himself. He was the first to admit his clothes weren't great, but he was comfortable, and that was what mattered to him. "My pets don't care how I look."

"And you clearly don't, either." She held up a pair of black jeans Maddox couldn't remember buying. "Okay, let's go with this, but don't let any of your cats and whatnot come close enough to get fur on it."

"Alice—"

"Nope. I'm not taking no for an answer. You're going to become a hermit if someone doesn't drag you out of here."

"I go to work every day."

"Yeah, and you work with animals. Not people. That doesn't count."

"I buy groceries."

She narrowed her eyes. "Look, we can do this my way, which is definitely the easiest way, or the harder way."

Maddox wasn't sure he wanted to know what that implied. He sighed heavily and took the jeans from her hands. "Fine."

She beamed. "Great! We're going to have fun, you'll see."

Maddox had a hard time believing that, but he didn't say it out loud. He didn't want to make Alice angry or sad. As long as she didn't try to get him to go dancing again in the next two or three months, he supposed he could do this.

CHAPTER TWO

Brandon grinned at Lee and Nathalie as he shook his hips. Lee grinned back, but Nathalie's attention was on something or someone behind Brandon. Brandon wasn't offended — the three of them were there to have fun, but also hopefully to pick up someone to take home, or in his and Lee's case, to a secluded place, because there was no way Brandon was going to take a guy back to his bedroom in the house he still shared with his mom. He'd managed to get out of talking to her today, but he knew his dad wanted to get this out of the way as soon as possible. Brandon wanted that, too, but he wasn't looking forward to the conversation he'd have to have with his mom.

Lee leaned closer. "You talked to your mom?"

Brandon rolled his eyes. "This isn't exactly the best place to talk about it!" He had to yell over the music, and he hoped Lee would get it and table the discussion for later. Couldn't he have brought this up in the car? And Brandon hated when his best friend seemed to read his mind. He loved Lee like a brother, but it made him uncomfortable.

Lee narrowed his eyes. "A yes or a no is fine with me."

"Tomorrow."

Lee didn't look convinced. "Just make sure you actually talk to her."

"I already talked to my dad, and he's okay with me moving. He wants to be there when I talk to my mom, so no worries there. There's no way I can get out of that conversation, no matter how much I want to."

Lee nodded. "Good."

"I feel like I should be offended by the lack faith you have in me."

Lee laughed. "You probably should, but it's only because I know you. You'd get out of it if you could. Don't try to deny it."

Brandon didn't. Instead, he stuck his tongue out at Lee and moved closer to him, putting one of his hands on Lee's waist and shaking his hips. They'd only ever been friends, but it was nice not to *have* to pick up someone. Lee was safe. He wouldn't expect Brandon to put out just because they were dancing together.

Brandon stopped dancing when his mouth felt like a desert. He needed a drink, and he needed it now.

He leaned closer to Lee again. "I'm going to grab some water. You want something?"

"Water, please."

Brandon looked around to see if he could find Nathalie, but she wasn't there. She was probably dancing with someone, which was exactly why they were there, so Brandon didn't worry. She was an adult, and she could take care of herself. She'd almost torn the head off the last guy who'd grabbed her ass.

Brandon made his way through the crowd toward the bar. There was a line, and he waited patiently, looking around. He recognized a few people in the club from the pack, but he didn't know them. They certainly weren't friends. He knew most of the pack members, but that didn't mean he was acquainted with everyone. The pack was too big for that, and Brandon tended to stick to his family and their friends.

"Hey, gorgeous. What are you drinking?"

Brandon turned toward the man. He'd never seen him, and while he'd agreed to come dancing with the idea of finding a guy to make-out with, he knew this wasn't the kind of guy he wanted in his life, not even to kiss and run. He wasn't sure what it was — the guy was tall and well-built, and Brandon would have been all over him usually — but he got weird vibes from him. "Water," he said, turning back to the bar and praying it was almost his turn.

"Water? That's boring."

"Maybe, but I'm thirsty."

"Let me buy you something else. A beer? A cocktail?"

"I'm underage. I'll stick to water, thanks." Brandon might have said yes any other day, but he didn't want to hurt his chances to move in with his dad by going home drunk tonight. His mom would kick his ass and decide he wasn't mature enough to be away from her. Then she'd kick his ass again and ground him even though he was eighteen and technically an adult.

"You look older." The guy looked Brandon up and down.

It made Brandon's skin crawl, and he could have kissed the bartender when he waved him forward. "Two bottles of water, please," he said leaning over the counter and handing the bartender the money.

The guy took it and put the bottles on the counter. Brandon reached for them, but the guy bugging him snatched one away. He cracked it open and held it out just as someone bumped against Brandon. Brandon jolted forward and gripped the counter so he wouldn't end up pressed against this guy. Some of the water sloshed out of the bottle and landed on Brandon's cheek.

He scrubbed it off with his hand and snatched the bottle from the guy, glaring at him. "What the fuck?"

The guy held his hands up. "I was just trying to help."

"I don't need help to open a bottle of water."

"Sorry, man. Didn't mean to piss you off." He held out the cap, and Brandon took it. He looked at the bottle, wondering if he should throw it away and get a new one, but when he looked at the bar, the line was longer than it had been the first time around. He didn't want to waste half an hour for a bottle of water. Besides, it wasn't like this guy had done anything to it. He'd just opened it and pissed Brandon off, but that was more because of Brandon than him. "Just stay away for me," Brandon snapped, not caring that he was rude.

He closed his bottle and went back to Lee. Nathalie was back, and she was dancing with two guys, her head thrown back and her long hair trailing down, sticking to her sweaty skin. Brandon smiled at the sight and handed Lee the still closed bottle of water. They both drank, and Brandon felt better once his throat wasn't parched anymore. He'd needed the water.

He threw the bottle away and went back to dancing with Lee. It wasn't long before a guy caught Lee's eyes, and Lee left Brandon behind with a wink and the promise to text him if he left with the guy. Brandon tried to lose himself to the music, but he didn't like dancing on his own, not at clubs anyway. Besides, he felt like he'd drunk a cocktail rather than water. His head started spinning, and the lights were weird. He didn't feel steady on his feet, either.

Brandon decided he was probably too warm and that some cool water splashed on his face would do him good. Nathalie was gone again, so he didn't stop on his way to the bathroom. People gave him a wide berth as if they thought he was drunk, and he couldn't deny he felt like he was. His thoughts were muddled, and he had to push through what felt like brain fog to make sure his feet went one in front of the other as he walked.

He was glad to see the bathroom was empty when he got there. It smelled terrible, and it was dirty, but he didn't care. He stuck his face under the faucet in one of the sinks and turned the water on, but it didn't help as much as he'd hoped.

"Hey there, gorgeous. What are you doing here all alone?"

Brandon swallowed. "Nothing. My friend is waiting for me."

"I don't think so. There's no one out there."

Brandon wanted to close his eyes. He *needed* to close them, but the guy from before walked toward him, and the only thing he managed to do was to lean heavily against the sink. He tried to wriggle away when the man grabbed his arm, but he might as well be trying to herd cats.

Shit. He'd been drugged, hadn't he? That was why he felt weak, too weak to resist when the man dragged him toward the closest bathroom stall.

Brandon knew what was going to happen, and no matter how hard he tried, he couldn't get away. The room spun around him, and the only fixed thing was the man who was pawing at his body through his clothes—for now. Brandon didn't doubt they wouldn't stay on him for much longer.

He opened his mouth to scream.

Maddox had enough of the loud music and the sweaty bodies around him, but he couldn't leave the club, not when Asher kept on making sure he was still there. "Shouldn't you be dancing with your mate?" Maddox asked. He had to repeat himself because Asher didn't hear him the first time around. Not surprising, considering the level of noise in the club. That was one of the reasons Maddox preferred his house or even the shelter.

Asher shrugged. "I will."

"You don't have to babysit me."

"Are you sure about that? Because I think you were about

to punch that guy on the nose earlier, and that wouldn't have ended well."

Maddox glared. "He squeezed my ass!"

"I know, and if it was just me here, I'd have *helped* you kick his ass. But this isn't the place."

Maddox took a deep breath, and a mix of strong perfumes and sweat hit his nose. He grimaced. He needed fresh air, not this. "I have to go to the bathroom." He wouldn't get fresh air there, but it would be better than what he was breathing now.

Hopefully.

Maddox was used to foul smells — the shelter didn't exactly smell of roses — so the bathroom would probably be familiar.

"I'll be here."

Maddox rolled his eyes. "Of course you will." He'd only half been hoping he would conveniently lose Asher in the club and be able to go home, but he knew better. Once Asher had his teeth in something, he didn't let go. The only thing he hadn't done it with was his relationship with Terry, and Maddox wasn't about to ask for details about that. It was none of his business, and he didn't *want* to know.

He left Asher behind, not missing the way Asher's attention was now on Terry, and headed toward the back of the club. He paused by the bar, wondering if he should get some water, but the line was long enough to scare him off. Hopefully, it would be shorter once he was done.

Maddox walked into the bathroom and blinked at the harsh white light. He frowned when something hit the door of one of the stalls behind him, but whatever was going on in there — and he had a good idea what it was — wasn't his business.

He went to the sink to rinse his hands, freezing when someone moaned *no*. It didn't sound like pleasure to Maddox. He bit his lower lip. What was going on in that stall? He could see two sets of feet under the door, and while it did look like one of them was trying to get away from the other, he couldn't be sure. Did it matter, though? If he interrupted two guys going at it, he'd apologize and leave, but he wouldn't be able to live with himself if he didn't do anything. He'd obsess over it until he found out what had happened, and if it was bad . . .

Maddox shook his head and turned to face the stall. It shook as if someone was trying to get out, and that was enough for him. He strode toward it and pulled, but of course, it was locked. "Come out of there!" he yelled.

There was a moment of silence before a man said, "Leave us alone."

"Not until I can be sure whatever you're doing is consensual."

"My boyfriend likes bathroom sex."

Somehow, Maddox doubted anyone liked bathroom sex, at least in this particular bathroom. He leaned closer to tell the guy to open again when a scent he hadn't smelled before hit his nose. Under the smell of urine, sweat, and bleach, was something—someone—who smelled of firewood and cinnamon, of *home*.

Maddox swallowed. His mate was behind that door, and he hoped it wasn't the guy trying to convince him that nothing weird was happening in the stall. "Open the fucking door right now. Unless you want me to call the police?" Maddox was going to call the cops anyway, but the guy inside the stall didn't need to know that.

The sound of the stall being unlocked made Maddox smile. A big man peered out, and Maddox didn't give him the time to close the door again. Hoping he wasn't assaulting his mate, he punched the guy in the face.

Blood spurted, and the guy swore. He raised both his

hands to his nose, and Maddox pushed the door open. It was hard to see the second man in there because he was behind this guy, leaning against the stall. He was sliding down, and when Maddox saw him, he swore. "What the fuck?" he grabbed the big guy by the collar and pulled him out of the stall. The man fell to his knees, but Maddox's attention was all on his mate.

The poor guy was almost on the floor by now, his knees not holding him up. His eyes were wide and unfocused, and even though he was scrambling to stay upright, he seemed to have the energy of a newborn kitten.

Maddox reached for him. His mate whimpered and tried to push him away, but he might as well have been a fly. Maddox gathered him into his arms and shuffled out of the stall. His mate's scent surrounded him, and he took it in. "Can you tell me your name?" he asked. He looked around for a place to put his mate down, but there was only the floor, and it was filthy. The man who'd been in the stall with Maddox's mate was gone, and right now, Maddox didn't care. He only cared about the man in his arms.

His mate looked more like a boy than a man, though. Maddox couldn't tell how old he was exactly, but it couldn't be much more than eighteen, if even that. His brown hair flopped on his forehead, and his eyes were brown, although they were fluttering closed right now. He'd relaxed as soon as Maddox had picked him up, and Maddox suspected it was because of his scent. Just like he could smell his mate, his mate could smell him, and it helped him feel safe.

Maddox's mate opened his mouth to say something, but the only thing that came out of it was a gurgle. Maddox huffed in frustration. He needed to call the cops, and ambulance, and possibly, his friends. *Shit.*

He raised a leg, balancing himself, and carefully reached into his jeans with his free hand. He hoped they weren't both about to topple to the floor as he took his phone out and speed-dialed Asher. He knew Asher's phone was in his pocket, so he'd feel it vibrate.

"Maddox?" Asher asked, his voice almost a yell over the music that blared both through Maddox's phone and outside the bathroom.

"Bathroom. Now."

Maddox dropped his phone onto the floor, but he didn't care. He cradled his mate against his chest and prayed Asher wouldn't take long. He breathed easier when Asher barged in, followed by the rest of their little group. His eyes widened when he saw Maddox's mate, but Terry intervened before Asher could start asking questions. "Ash, call the cops. I'm calling an ambulance. Can you tell me what happened, Maddox?"

"I don't know. I came in, and strange noises were coming from one of the stalls. I knocked and told the guys to come out, then punched the one who opened the stall door when I realized he had my mate in there with him. I think he's been drugged."

Terry didn't even pause at the admission that the man in Maddox's arms was his mate. "Okay."

Maddox wasn't sure what to do. Other people came to the bathroom, but Alice and Gabriel kept them out. They only let in a guy, and Maddox thought he recognized him from the pack. "Are you a pack member?" he asked.

"Yes, and so is Brandon. What happened to him?"

"Some guy was assaulting him, and I think he's been drugged."

The man wrung his hands. "I shouldn't have let him go to the bar on his own. Or to the bathroom."

"What's your name?"

"Lee."

"Lee, call his parents and tell them to meet us at the hospital, okay?" Maddox knew that was where the ambulance would take them. Hopefully, Brandon wouldn't have to stay for long, and if he did, Dallas would probably be able to move him to the pack's infirmary.

Lee nodded. He didn't seem to be able to look away from Brandon, not even when the EMTs arrived and Maddox had to let go of him.

He had no idea what the EMTs were doing or what they were saying, so he stepped away when they moved to get Brandon out. Terry pushed him back, though, saying," They're mates," when one of the EMTs protested.

That seemed to do it. They accepted Maddox's presence as normal as they headed to the ambulance, even though Maddox had no idea what he was doing there.

Brandon was his mate, but they didn't even know each other. What the fuck was Maddox supposed to do?

The memory of hands on his body jerked Brandon awake. He scrambled back even before realizing he was in a hospital bed.

His mom whimpered and reached for him. "Brandon?"

Brandon relaxed and blinked. "Mom? Dad?" Even Matt was there, which meant that whatever had happened hadn't been good.

His dad reached for his hand and squeezed it. "How are you feeling?"

"I have a headache." And he was fucking confused. Why had he woken up afraid? "What happened?"

"You don't remember?"

"Not really."

His dad nodded curtly. "What *do* you remember?"

Brandon frowned. "I went to the club with Lee and Nathalie."

"You did."

"I remember dancing, buying a bottle of water." *What else?* "A man?"

Brandon's mom sobbed. "He drugged you."

Brandon couldn't remember that. His head hurt more when he tried to focus, but he hated feeling like he was missing a part of his life, no matter how bad it had been. "There was a man. He smelled good." He'd smelled like Brandon's mate, but Brandon had no idea if he'd been the one to drug him, and he didn't want his parents to freak out.

They didn't. His mom was still crying, but his dad had relaxed, although only marginally. Matt looked like he wanted to leave the room, but Brandon knew it was because he still wasn't comfortable being a stepfather, especially not to two teenage boys. Still, he was there, and that meant a lot to Brandon.

His dad cleared his throat. "That was your mate."

Brandon's brain had trouble working through that statement. "My mate?"

Brandon's father looked toward the door, and Brandon realized a man was standing there. He hadn't noticed him before, and he wasn't surprised. If Matt looked like he wanted to leave, this man looked like he wanted to run away screaming bloody murder and never look back. Was he Brandon's mate? That didn't tell Brandon what had happened, although he doubted his parents would be okay with his mate standing there if he'd been the one who'd drugged him.

When Brandon's mate didn't say anything, Brandon's dad cleared his throat. "This is Maddox. He walked into the bathroom at the club before the man who drugged you could . . . take advantage of you. And yes, he's your mate, or at least that's what he told us."

Brandon wanted to sniff Maddox, but he wasn't about to

ask. "I think he is." Maybe. Brandon didn't think Maddox would have a reason to lie, though, so he was pretty sure this really was happening.

He rubbed his face. He wanted to go home and sleep for a week, but he also wanted to spend time with Maddox and talk to him, and he *needed* to know what had happened. "I was drugged?"

"Yes."

There was only one reason people were drugged in clubs, and the words his dad had said earlier didn't leave questions. "Where is he? The guy who tried to, you know?"

"Maddox was focused on you, so he didn't notice the man leaving. But the police were called, and I'm sure they're doing everything they can to find him and put him behind bars," Brandon's mom said. She leaned closer. "And as soon as the doctors say you can leave, I'm taking you home."

Brandon had to press his lips together not to groan. He hated what had happened tonight, both because he felt violated and like he needed a scalding shower and because he knew his mom was freaking out. She'd already been hovering before. There was no way she'd let him out of her sight now. "I feel okay." Brandon needed a shower and his pajamas.

"You can't even remember what happened. You are *not* okay, Brandon."

Brandon knew she was right. He might feel decent right now, but that wasn't going to last.

A quick knock on the door made him look up. Patrick peeked in, tightly smiling when he saw Brandon was awake. He opened the door and stepped in, followed by a nurse who looked like he might clock Patrick in the face. "What are you doing? I told you he needs more time to rest."

"He's awake."

"That doesn't mean he's well enough to answer your

questions, Detective." The nurse stopped at the foot of Brandon's bed and put his hands on his hips, glaring at Patrick. "You can come back tomorrow."

"The sooner I can talk to Brandon, the better chance I will have to find the man who did this to him," Patrick pointed out.

It had taken Brandon a moment to realize he was there for professional reasons. He was mildly surprised, since Patrick was a detective, but he supposed Kameron had asked him to help. Being part of the pack meant being part of a big family, even when you didn't talk to all of its members, and in this case, Brandon *had* talked to Patrick in the past. His dad was friends with Grey, Patrick's mate

"I'm sure it can wait," the nurse insisted.

"I'm okay," Brandon said. He might as well talk with Patrick right away. "I can talk to him."

The nurse turned to face Brandon. "Are you sure? I should call the doctor and have him examine you."

"That's fine, but I *want* to talk to Detective Novak. Please. I want the guy who did this to me to get caught." Because there was no way this was the first time he'd done it. Brandon might not remember most of what had happened, but he did remember that.

The nurse frowned, and Brandon expected him to say no, but he nodded. "All right. But I'm calling the doctor, and as soon as she gets here, the detective has to go."

"That's fine," Patrick said. "I need to talk to other people anyway."

The nurse left, and Maddox moved after him, but Patrick stopped him. "Stay here. We can leave together once I'm done with Brandon."

Dammit. Brandon wanted to talk to Maddox. They were mates, yet they hadn't even talked yet. His parents had no doubt had a conversation with him since he was there and they knew they were mates, and Brandon hated that. He didn't have a choice, though, and he suspected his mom would push for him to go back to sleep as soon as Patrick was gone.

He sighed. "I don't remember much," he told Patrick.

Patrick sat on the edge of the mattress and patted Brandon's foot. "That's okay. I know you were drugged, so I'm not surprised. But every single detail can help."

Brandon nodded and closed his eyes. He leaned back against his pillow and tried to think through his headache and the mess of feelings. "I was at the club with Lee and Nathalie. We were having fun, dancing, and I got thirsty. I went to the bar. I got . . . two bottles of water, I think. One for me, and one for Lee." Brandon opened his eyes. "Is Lee okay?"

"He's fine. He wasn't drugged. Do you remember anyone at the bar? The bartender said the bottles were both sealed when he gave them to you, so whoever drugged you had to do it between the time you left the bar and the time you got to Lee."

Brandon's mind felt like it was muddled, but he could do this. He had to. "There was a guy at the bar. He was tall. I didn't want to talk to him, but he was pushy." Brandon frowned. "He took my bottle, I think."

Patrick straightened. "He did?"

"Yeah. But he gave it back."

"Is it possible that he slipped the drug into it then?"

Brandon opened his mouth to say it wasn't. But he remembered being pushed. He'd lost eye contact with the bottle, but it had been so fast. "Maybe? Someone pushed me, and I looked away. It was only for a few seconds, though."

"It wouldn't take much more than that. What did the man say? Why did he take the bottle from you?"

"He opened it." Brandon felt like he was about to puke all

over Patrick. "He took the bottle and opened it. He made it look like he was trying to be nice, and I brushed it off. I didn't think anything of it."

"What happened next?"

"I don't know." And no matter how hard Brandon tried to remember, he only got impressions and vague images. "I went to the bathroom, I think?"

"That's where Maddox found you. Do you think you can identify the man who drugged you?"

"Maybe." Brandon tried to describe him as well as he could. "He was tall, with dark, short hair."

Patrick smiled. "All right. I'm going to let you rest now. I'd like you to come to the station tomorrow if you feel up to it. I have enough witnesses to have an idea who this man is."

Brandon wanted to say no. He never wanted to see that guy again. But he couldn't stop thinking about what would have happened if his brother had been in his place, or Lee. "I'll come," he said before his mom could forbid it. He owed it to whoever else this guy had drugged and assaulted.

And he owed it to himself.

Maddox rushed out of the hospital room. He ignored his caracal, who wasn't happy with him, but it wanted some time to relax as much as Maddox did. Of course, if the caracal had his way, they'd relax *with* Brandon rather than away from him, but Brandon was still recuperating, and they hadn't even talked yet. Besides, Maddox wasn't sure what to think of Brandon or of the fact that he'd met his mate and that Brandon was so young. God, Maddox had never expected his mate would be ten years younger than him. It wasn't a lot, considering they were shifters, but Brandon was so young. Had he even finished high school yet? There was no way he was happy to find his mate at only eighteen.

"Maddox? I need to talk to you."

Maddox froze at the sound of Patrick's voice and sighed. He'd known he wouldn't be able to get out of this, and honestly, he didn't want to. His blood boiled at the thought of what that man had been trying to do to his mate—of what he *would* have done if Maddox hadn't accidentally walked in on him.

He faced Patrick. He was glad Patrick was the one who would be taking care of this. He was part of the pack, of the family, and he'd make sure the asshole paid. "I don't have a lot to say."

Patrick arched a brow. "Your mate was attacked and almost raped."

"I'm aware of that, trust me." Maddox doubted he'd ever be able to forget what he'd walked in on. Even if he and Brandon never ended up together, that situation would be forever branded in his brain.

Patrick nodded. "Then you won't have a problem telling me what happened?"

Maddox sighed. "I don't. I wish I could never think about it again, though."

Patrick's expression softened. "I realize that. I don't know what I would have done if I'd been in your situation. The best thing to do right now though is to help me get that guy and put him behind bars. Then he'll never be able to do what he did to anyone else, and he'll pay for what happened with Brandon."

Maddox leaned against the wall and crossed his arms over his chest. "Will you even be able to get anything to stick? He didn't rape Brandon." And thank God for that.

"Because you intervened. You're a witness to what was happening, or what was about to happen, though."

"Not really. They were in one of the stalls."

"But you were worried enough to intervene."

Maddox sighed. "Yeah, I was. Okay, what do you want to know?"

"Just go over what happened, please."

Maddox knew he could do that. Every single second was fresh, and it was hell. "I went to the bathroom. I wanted some time away from the noise and the smells. The bathroom wasn't the greatest place to do that, but it was something, and I couldn't leave without my friends."

"You'll give me a list of the people you were with later, all right?"

"Sure."

"So you went to the bathroom."

"Yeah. It was empty, or so I thought, but then I heard noise coming from one of the stalls. I didn't think it was my business, especially when I noticed two pairs of feet from under the door. But then I heard one of them, Brandon, say *no,* and it didn't sound like it was the kind of *no* you know is really a *yes.* That's when I paid attention."

"And when you decided to help."

"Kinda. I wasn't sure it was the right thing to do, and I didn't want to intrude if they were just, you know, having sex, but I thought interrupting wouldn't be as bad as ignoring it and suspecting someone got hurt, especially when it looked like one of the guys was trying to get out. I knocked, and when the guy opened to tell me he and his boyfriend were having fun, I smelled Brandon."

"And you realized you were mates."

"Yeah. But that wasn't why I pulled the other guy out. I managed to look around him, and I saw Brandon. He couldn't even stand on his own, and I knew there was no way it was consensual, not when it looked like he was drunk or drugged. I dragged the other guy out of the stall and grabbed Brandon."

"You don't know what happened to that other guy?"

"It's obvious he left. I was focused on Brandon, so I didn't even think about trying to stop him." Maddox rubbed the back of his neck. "I'm sorry."

"You did what you had to do. Can you identify the man? Because I'm not sure I can rely on Brandon's testimony, not when he can't remember much. I'll check the CCTV, of course, but that will only place the guy at the club, not in the bathroom with Brandon."

"Probably."

"Great."

Maddox did his best to remember every detail he could about what the guy looked like. He even added that he'd punched him so that Patrick knew to look for someone with a black eye. He was glad when Patrick nodded and closed his notebook, though. It was going on morning, and he needed to work tomorrow. His pets were bound to be anxious about the fact that he wasn't home yet, and he needed sleep.

"I'll contact you if I need anything else," Patrick said.

"Of course."

Maddox moved to leave, but another voice stopped him. "Maddox?"

Maddox almost groaned. He managed to stifle the sound, though. He didn't want Brandon's parents to think he had something against them. "Yes?"

Brandon's father smiled at him. "I just wanted to thank you for what you did."

"You already thanked me." That had been one of the most awkward and uncomfortable moments in Maddox's life. Brandon's friend had called his parents, but Maddox had been the one who'd met them in the waiting room at the hospital. He'd had to explain what had happened, and that included telling them that he and Brandon were mates. He could have skipped that bit, but both he and his caracal cat had wanted to be able to find out how Brandon was. Besides, they would probably have found out once Brandon had woken up, since it looked like Brandon knew it even though he'd been drugged when they'd met. And even without knowing they were mates, they might have tried to include Maddox.

Brandon's father's smile widened. "I know I did, but trust me, I'm going to thank you plenty of times still. This isn't something I can forget."

"I understand." What was Maddox supposed to say to that?

"You can stay, you know? I don't know when Brandon will be allowed to leave, but you can wait with us."

Maddox was torn. On the one hand, he wanted to say yes, but on the other, there was no way he'd stick around, and it wasn't only because he had to go to work later. Having to stick around with Brandon and his family, possibly answering questions and being stared at, was Maddox's definition of torture. "I have to go to work in a few hours, and I have pets to take care of at home."

"Oh, of course. I just thought you might be able to take the day off since Brandon is your mate. But you work at the shelter, right?"

"Yes. There are a few volunteers and other workers there, but I don't like to take time off when I don't have to. The animals can't afford *not* to be fed or cleaned."

"I understand. But feel free to come over when you're off work later, or whenever you're free. I'm sure Brandon will be happy to see you and to start getting to know you."

Maddox's stomach churned. He couldn't tell Brandon's father that he wasn't sure getting to know his son was a good idea. Hell, he wasn't sure how he felt about any of this, and he wasn't going to find out with no sleep. But if there was one thing he was sure of, it was that he wasn't about to trust anyone with his heart, not even his mate. Brandon might be a shifter, but that didn't mean he couldn't leave Maddox and hurt him. He might not *want* a mate right now, not at eighteen, and Maddox would understand. "Thank you."

"Go get some sleep. You look like you need it."

Maddox snorted. "I feel like I need it, too."

A shower, sleep, and not thinking about what had happened. Maddox didn't want anything more than that.

CHAPTER THREE

Brandon stretched and smiled at the ceiling. God, it felt good to wake up in his bed, especially after the night he'd had. He wasn't sure what time it was, and he didn't care. He didn't have to go to school today. He *did* need to go into town to talk to Patrick like they'd agreed on yesterday, but that could wait a few hours.

He stopped smiling. It was good to be in his bed, but he wished he hadn't had nightmares. He couldn't even remember what had happened to him, so how could he be dreaming about it? He had no clue, yet there he was. He wanted to burrow into his bed and stay there for the rest of the day, hopefully without more nightmares, but he knew better. His mom would be there to get him out of bed soon. He was surprised she hadn't come around yet, but he supposed he got a pass after yesterday.

Both his parents had been frightened, and he understood that. He was fine, though. He was probably going to have nightmares for a while, but really, that was nothing next to what could have happened. He was lucky Maddox had walked into the bathroom when he had.

Brandon rolled to his side and hugged his pillow.

Why hadn't Maddox stayed? Brandon's dad had told him Maddox had to work today and that he worked at the shelter, so it made sense that he'd gone to bed, but they hadn't even talked. It was almost as if Maddox had run away the moment he'd been sure Brandon would be okay.

That couldn't be right, though. They were mates. Maddox

40

had been worried.

Okay, so the circumstance in which they'd met wasn't the best. It was one of the worst. Brandon hated what he'd gone through, but he didn't remember most of it. Maddox did, though. He'd been right there, a witness to what had happened and what *might* have happened. Maybe he'd freaked out? Brandon would have. He wasn't sure he would have run as soon as possible, but he wasn't Maddox.

He knew Maddox was a pack member, so he wasn't too worried about finding him. It wasn't like Maddox was hiding from him. He'd just needed sleep because he had to work today.

Brandon knew he wouldn't be able to fall asleep again, mostly because now that he was awake, he wouldn't be able to stop thinking. It wouldn't be a bad thing if he could think only of Maddox, but he doubted he'd be able to push away the memories of what had happened last night or his nightmares, so he rolled out of bed.

His mouth felt like something had crawled in it and died even though he'd brushed his teeth before going to bed, so he hurried into the bathroom. He hoped he'd feel better once he was showered and dressed. He still smelled faintly like the hospital.

Maybe that was the reason Maddox had left, or one reason, anyway. Brandon hadn't been at his best last night. Could Maddox have left to give Brandon time to wrap his mind around the evening and get better? Brandon wished he'd had his mate with him, but it wasn't like they'd talked about it. Maddox might have thought Brandon would feel better if he didn't see him like that or something. Not that it would have changed anything, since Maddox was the one who'd walked in on that guy assaulting Brandon, but still.

That thought made Brandon smile, and he kept on smiling until he got downstairs and heard both his parents were in the kitchen. They weren't yelling, but their voices were sharp and angry.

"You can't keep him under a glass dome," his dad said.

"I'm not. I just want him to be safe."

"I know that. I want the same thing. And don't give me that look, Justine. We might not be married anymore, but that doesn't change the fact that I'm Brandon and Jason's father. Whatever you feel about that, I have as much right as you to make decisions for the kids. In this case, I think you're exaggerating."

"Exaggerating? He was almost *raped*, Colin. Raped. He was drugged, and God knows what that man would have done to him if Maddox hadn't walked into the bathroom just then."

Brandon's stomach churned. He might have been thinking the same thing only moments before, but he knew his mom would use it to try to keep him in the house and in her sight as much as possible. He even understood the reason behind it—no one wanted their kid to go through what he'd gone through—but he'd already felt sheltered before. If she went on like she'd been doing, or worse, if she became even more mother hen, he was going to feel trapped in his own house, and that wasn't something he wanted.

"I know. Trust me, my mind went over all the possible scenarios and threw them back to me last night while I slept. I'm terrified something is going to happen to Brandon again, or to Jason. But that doesn't mean we have to lock them up."

"I'm not going to lock him up."

"You just said you're not sure he should go back to school, Justine. That's not locking him up, but it's damn close, and I'm not going to let you do that to him. He's already been through enough."

Brandon's mom snorted. "It's easy for you to say that. You have your new life, with your house and your mate."

There was a moment of silence, and when Brandon's father spoke next, Brandon could hear the anger in his voice. "Are you saying that because I met Matt and bonded with him, I don't love or care about my sons as much as I used to?"

Shit. Brandon didn't want his parents to fight.

He stepped into the kitchen, clearing his throat. His mom and dad were both sitting at the kitchen table, and they turned to look at him. They both smiled, and Brandon's mom was on her feet and hugging him before he could say anything. He hugged her back, closing his eyes at her familiar, soothing scent.

"How did you sleep, sweetheart?" she asked.

"Okay. What's going on?"

She shook her head. "Nothing for you to worry about."

Brandon couldn't tell her he knew what she was hiding unless he wanted to confess that he'd been eavesdropping, and he wasn't about to do that.

"Do you want breakfast?" she asked.

"I'm not really hungry."

She frowned. "Are you sure? You'll feel better with some food in you."

Brandon's phone rang, and he could have kissed whoever it was. "I'm fine, Mom. I need to take this."

It was Patrick. "We got a few guys in. Are you up for a line-up?" he asked.

Brandon blinked. "So fast?" He'd expected this to take weeks, if not longer.

"Maddox gave us a great description."

Brandon's heart beat faster. "He did?" Of course he had. He'd seen the guy in the stall with Brandon, and unlike Brandon, he remembered everything.

"Yes. And of course, the club gave us the CCTV."

"I can be there in half an hour."

Brandon's mom grimaced, but he ignored her. He already knew she'd rather have him stay home, or maybe worse, go with him. "My father can come with me, right?" he asked. He hated how hurt his mom looked, but it was either exclude her from this or have her hover even more.

"Of course."

Brandon was glad he'd be able to do something. He wanted the guy to pay, even though he didn't remember anything.

The line-up was weird. Brandon had seen plenty of them on TV, so he knew how it worked. Still, seeing the man who'd drugged him, even behind the glass and knowing he couldn't see Brandon, wasn't easy. Brandon was glad when Patrick patted his shoulder and said he could leave, especially since his mom had decided to come with them and had been hovering just like he'd known she would. "You did a good job."

"I just told you who hurt me."

"I know, but it takes courage to face what happened and the man who did it. Not everyone has it."

Brandon wasn't sure he would have if things had been worse, if the guy had managed to do what he'd intended to do. Things were hard enough to deal with as it was. How much worse would they have been if the man had raped Brandon like he'd been planning to? Brandon wouldn't have to find out, but he knew he was one of the lucky ones.

"I'll find you!"

The scream made Brandon jerk. He moved closer to his dad, and his dad wrapped an arm around his shoulders, while his mom stepped in front of him. She looked ready to tear someone's head off, and for once, Brandon was glad for her presence. The man Brandon had identified had moved away from the others and was up to the glass now. Brandon knew he couldn't see him, but he was still freaked out because the man seemed to be looking right at him.

"I'll find you, and I'll kill you, you bitch," the man growled.

Brandon buried his face against his father's chest and prayed that wouldn't happen.

Maddox rubbed the cat's head and wondered what they could call her. She was a pretty white thing with a fluffy tail, and she looked like she should have a royal name. Queen Victoria, maybe?

"You are *not* taking this one home," Asher said from behind Maddox.

Maddox sighed. "I know." He gave Queen Victoria one last rub and stood. Asher was leaning against the door frame with his arms crossed over his chest and a stubborn expression on his face.

Maddox had been avoiding him all morning, but that was clearly over. Maddox wasn't surprised. He was lucky Asher hadn't pounced earlier, although that might be because he hadn't been able to find him or because someone had dumped Queen Victoria in front of the shelter and Maddox had been busy with her, helping the veterinarian and washing her.

"You still want to take her."

It wasn't a question, but Maddox would rather answer that than the questions Asher had for him about last night. "Well, yes, but she still has a chance to find a good home. She just got here, and she's gorgeous."

"Let's hope she finds a family, then."

"You could take her."

"Nope. I already have enough on my hands at home. And you're not taking her, either. I'll make sure she finds a home that's not yours."

Maddox frowned. "Why are you so against me having pets?"

"I'm not against you having pets. I'm against you having more pets than friends. And I wouldn't care if I didn't know they're a substitute for the human relationships you work so hard to avoid."

"I don't know what you're talking about," Maddox said, pushing past Asher to leave the cats' room.

"Bullshit. What happened last night, Maddox? Who was that guy?"

Maddox stopped. He was surprised Asher wasn't already asking why Maddox hadn't told him Brandon was his mate and whatnot. "Didn't Terry tell you?"

"He told me he was your mate, but that's all I know, and I don't know if I should believe it because you'd have told me if it was, right? And you wouldn't be here."

Maddox walked into the break room and flopped into one of the chairs. He rubbed his face. God, he needed more sleep. He'd only gotten a few hours, and even those hadn't been restful. His brain wouldn't turn off, and he'd kept thinking about Brandon and what had happened to him.

"You need coffee," Asher declared.

Maddox wasn't sure why he wasn't pushing for more answers, but he wasn't going to complain, not when Asher was offering coffee and giving him a few minutes of peace.

They didn't talk while Asher brewed a fresh pot. He even poured Maddox a cup, adding the creamer Maddox preferred. Maddox took the steaming mug with a smile and closed his eyes as he sipped, trying not to burn his tongue.

"Ready to talk about it?" Asher asked after a few moments.

Maddox groaned. "No." He didn't think he'd ever be ready to listen to what Asher had to say.

Of course, Asher ignored his words and went ahead. "So that guy last night was your mate?"

"You already know that. Why are you asking?"

"Just wanted to be sure. Because whatever happened to him looked bad, so I'm not sure what to think of the fact that instead of being with him right now you're here washing cats and thinking about taking them home."

"I am *not* taking Queen Victoria home."

Asher chuckled. "Yet you named her like you did with your cats."

"She needed a name."

"All right, she did. But let's get back to your mate. Why aren't you with him, Maddox? You know everyone would have stepped up to take your shift today if you'd just asked, even if it hadn't been because you had to be with your mate."

Maddox wrapped his hands around his mug and stared at the liquid. "I know. I'm okay, though. I don't need to take time off."

"How is he?"

"He's fine." Or he was when Maddox had last seen him last night. He didn't have a way to contact Brandon, and he wasn't sure he wanted one. There was no way Asher would take that for an answer, though.

"You called him?"

"Asher. Can we not talk about this? We're at work. I told you Brandon is fine. That's all you need to know."

Asher jerked back. He was hurt, and Maddox hated that he'd been the one to do that. He hadn't meant to.

He sighed. "I'm sorry."

Asher nodded. "It's okay. I guess it's none of my business."

"It is. I'm just being an asshole. But then you shouldn't be surprised. You know me."

"I do, and I know you're being an asshole because you're scared. I can't force you to talk, but Maddox, you should know by now that I only want what's best for you."

"And you think my mate is what's best for me."

"I don't know. It would be for a lot of people."

"I guess. It was for you, wasn't it?"

"It's a bit more complicated than that. I knew who my mate was for a long time before I told Terry. You know that." Asher licked his lips. "How long have you known about Brandon?"

They were going to do this. Maddox was going to have to tell Asher about Brandon and his feelings and whatever. He owed it to Asher, who was always there for him when he needed. Besides, it might do him good to talk about it. Not talking about Brandon didn't seem to do much more than freaking him out and worrying him. "I met him last night in that bathroom."

Asher sucked in a breath. "Really? Shit. I'm sorry."

Maddox shrugged. "What for? It's not like you chose to have me and Brandon meet that way."

"What happened when you got to the hospital?"

"The doctors took him away, and I had what was probably the most awkward conversation of my life with Brandon's parents. They freaked out in the beginning, so I had to tell them I was Brandon's mate. That's when they started thanking me. They insisted I stay around until Brandon woke up."

"And you did?"

"Yeah. I had to talk to the cops."

Asher arched a brow. "That's the only reason you stayed?"

"You know it's not." Because no matter what Maddox thought of Brandon being his mate, that didn't change the fact that he was and that Maddox wanted him to be okay.

"What are you going to do?"

Maddox had been asking himself that since last night. "I don't know."

"What do you *want* to do?"

"I don't know." Maddox first instinct was to go on with his life as if he'd never met Brandon, but he knew he couldn't. It wouldn't be fair to Brandon, who had no idea how messed up Maddox was.

"Yeah, you do. You want to shut him out, don't you?"

Maddox glared at Asher. "You think you know me that well."

"That's because I do. We've been friends for a while, and I have eyes. I see how you isolate yourself, and I know it's because of what happened with your parents. People can't reject you and hurt you if you don't let them close."

"Since when are you a psychologist?"

"I'm not, but it doesn't take one to see you, Maddox. And I even understand why you feel that way. Your parents were assholes, and instead of taking care of you like they should have, they threw you out. They weren't parents. They were people who happened to reproduce. And I know what they did will always hurt you. But, Maddox, you've been living with the pack for twelve years, since you were sixteen. Don't you know we'll never kick you out?"

Maddox did. His brain was aware of that. The pack didn't kick out people, not unless they did something horrible, and Maddox had no intention of doing anything like that. But knowing that didn't help his heart believing it. Besides, the pack meant less to him than his few friends, and they would mean less than his mate if Maddox ever let himself open up to Brandon.

Maddox finished his coffee. He didn't know what to tell Asher, but he didn't want his friend to insist, not right now. He knew better than to think that Asher wasn't going to bring this up again, and soon. "He's too young."

Asher blinked. "What?"

"Brandon. He's only eighteen. There's no way he wants to be with me, mate or no mate."

"You can't know that. You haven't talked to him." Asher grabbed Maddox's hand. "Look, just promise me you'll talk to him. Give him a chance to get to know you. Even if he's not ready for anything, he has the right to know what's going on. Whatever you think of it or feel about it, you two are mates, and that means something."

"Are you going to kick my ass if I don't?"

Asher grinned. "Damn right I will. I know you, Maddox. Sooner or later, you're going to regret not doing the right thing, but by then, it might be too late."

Asher was right. He often was. "All right. I promise I'll talk to him. I promised you I'd give him a chance, didn't I? So I will."

Brandon grinned at Lee and Nathalie and waved them in. Lee pulled Brandon into a bear hug that pushed the air out of Brandon's lungs. They weren't usually so touchy-feely, but Brandon hugged him back. He'd texted Lee last night after the doctor had told him he could go home, so both he and Nathalie knew he was okay, but seeing him with their own eyes had to be different.

When Lee let go, Nathalie replaced him. Her eyes were red and swollen, and her hair looked like she hadn't looked at herself in the mirror this morning. However, she felt so good in Brandon's arms. She and Lee helped ground Brandon in the present, and he needed that, what with his mind always slipping toward last night's memories.

"You scared us to death," Nathalie scolded him.

He smiled. "I know. Trust me, I would have done without

it if I could have."

Nathalie's lower lip trembled. "God, Bran. I'm so sorry."

He rubbed her arm. "You have nothing to be sorry for. It wasn't your fault."

"No, the fault is all on that asshole," Lee spat out.

Brandon couldn't help but smile. "Yeah, it was, and he's behind bars right now, so you don't have to worry about him."

"Are you sure you're okay?" Nathalie's voice still wavered, and Brandon wasn't sure what he could do to make her feel better. He felt the way she looked—shaky and unsteady, as though if he wasn't careful his life would come down around him. He knew it wouldn't, but he supposed it would take him a few days at least to start working through what had happened.

"Who was that guy who went with you to the hospital?" Lee asked as they climbed upstairs to Brandon's room. "Someone said he was your mate, so the EMTs let him go with you. I should have told them it was bullshit and gone in his place, but I was freaking out, and Nathalie was still in the club."

Brandon cleared his throat. "Actually, he *is* my mate."

Lee stopped right there on the stairs. He grabbed Brandon's jeans and pulled him back, almost making him fall. "Your *what*?"

Brandon laughed and freed himself. "Come on. Let's go to my room." His mom was in the house, and while she knew about Maddox, Brandon didn't want her to hear his conversation with his two best friends.

He made sure his bedroom door was closed, then he flopped onto his bed. He winced, the bruises on his waist making themselves known, but he pushed them and the memories they brought with them away to focus on Maddox. "His name is Maddox, and yeah, he's my mate. I found out last night when I woke up in the hospital."

Lee sat cross-legged in front of Brandon, while Nathalie had taken the desk chair. They both leaned closer now. "What happened?" Nathalie asked. She didn't look as haunted as she had before, and Brandon hoped that the bit of gossiping would help her.

"Well, you know what that guy did to me. When I woke up in the hospital, my parents were there, and so was Maddox. They explained what had happened because I didn't remember most of it. I still don't, to be honest, but I'm glad for that. They also told me Maddox had been the one who'd helped me, and that we were mates."

Lee waved his hand. "We get that, but what happened with *Maddox*? What did you do? Did you go home with him last night?"

"Of course not. I came home with my mom and stayed in bed until lunchtime."

"What about Maddox?" Nathalie asked.

"I don't know. He left the hospital last night after talking with Patrick."

"And?"

"And nothing."

She frowned. "Why didn't you call him?"

Brandon looked down at his hands. "I don't have his number. And I don't know where he lives or much of anything about him. I only know he's a pack member."

Lee wrinkled his nose. "So you don't know how to find him? Why did he leave anyway? Doesn't he want you?"

Brandon shrugged and tried not to think about that possibility. "He was probably as freaked out as I was. I mean, he finds his mate in a club's bathroom being assaulted, takes him to the hospital because he's been drugged, meets his mate's parents before they even have a chance to talk, and has to give the police a statement. It's not exactly the best way to meet."

"Maybe. Still."

"What did he look like?" Nathalie asked.

Brandon smiled at the memory of Maddox. They might not have had the chance to talk, but he'd looked. "He's tall, not very muscled, on the thin side. Well, from what I saw with his clothes on, anyway. He has brown hair cut short. I don't know about his eyes because he stayed by the door. He's hot, though."

Nathalie rolled her eyes. "That's not going to help. Most people in the pack are hot."

Lee grimaced. "Eww. Please, tell me that doesn't include my parents or my brothers."

Nathalie grinned. "I don't know. I mean, Jamie is—"

Lee slapped his hands over his ears. "Nope. Not listening to that. But you know, I recognized Maddox."

It was Brandon's turn to lean closer. "You do?"

"I think I've seen him around. He has dogs?"

"I have no idea."

"Well, I'm pretty sure he does. He always takes them for walks around the playground and the fire pit. Maybe he's there right now."

"Or maybe he's still at work," Nathalie pointed out.

"It won't cost anything to go there and see if we can find him, though." Lee smiled. "Come on. It'll do you good to leave this house."

He didn't have to tell Brandon twice, because Brandon couldn't wait to get out. His mom had been stuck to him since he'd come back from the station. He was lucky she hadn't snuck into his bedroom along with Lee and Nathalie.

The three of them put their shoes on and left the bedroom. Brandon was laughing at something Nathalie had said when they got to the front door—and found his mom there waiting for him. "Hey, Mom."

"What's happening?"

"Nothing. We're just going out."

"No, you're not."

Brandon blinked. "What?"

"You're not leaving this house, Brandon, not after what happened last night."

"We're only going to the fire pit."

"I don't care where you're planning to go. Lee and Nathalie can go without you because you're staying here."

Brandon wished she'd taken him to the side to tell him instead of doing it in front of his friends. "Why don't you wait for me outside?" he asked Lee and Nathalie.

Lee nodded. "Just let us know if you're not coming."

"I am. I just need a moment."

"Brandon!" his mom yelled.

Brandon winced. *Shit.* He didn't want to do this, especially not now. "What, Mom?"

"I already told you, you're not leaving the house."

"Mom, I'm only going to the fire pit, and if it makes you feel better, Lee and Nathalie are going to stick with me. We're going to try to find Maddox. I promise I won't leave pack territory if it makes you feel better."

She crossed her arms over her chest. "I know he's your mate, but he can come here if you want to meet him. I'm not letting you out of my sight."

Brandon understood she was doing this because she was scared for him and she didn't want anything like that to happen again, but he didn't think it was the right way. "You're not going to be able to keep me here, Mom. I have school on Monday."

"I'll drive you there. I'll also pick you up."

"Am I grounded?" He couldn't remember the last time he'd been grounded.

"No. I'm trying to keep you safe."

"And you're doing that by locking me in the house? Come on, Mom. I'm eighteen. I can take care of myself."

"Like you did last night?"

That hurt. "Are you saying it was my fault I was drugged?"

At least she looked sorry. "Of course not."

"Then why don't you trust me to go to the fucking fire pit? Besides, it's not like you can stop me. I'm eighteen."

"And you still live under my roof. If you don't like my rules, you can—"

"I want to move in with Dad and Matt."

Brandon's mom snapped her mouth shut. Brandon regretted telling her he wanted to move this way, but it was out now.

His phone rang before he could explain, or at least try to. He groaned, but he took it out, hoping it might by some miracle be Maddox.

It was Patrick.

"Brandon?" he said when Brandon answered.

"Yes?"

"Where are you?"

"At home."

"All right. Don't leave pack territory."

"What? Why?" Was he going to try to ground Brandon like his mom was?

"The man who drugged and assaulted you escaped."

Maddox had made his decision. He was going to talk to Brandon as soon as he wrapped his mind around everything and found out what he was ready for. He wasn't sure how long *that* would take, but he doubted Brandon had even noticed he wasn't around. He probably had other things to focus on right now.

Maddox dropped his groceries into his truck and hesitated. His break was almost over, but he still had time to grab a coffee. He could get a cup at the shelter, but he'd have to make do with what they had there. If he stopped at the coffee shop, though, he could get a caramel latte.

Decision made, he turned to walk to the coffee shop, but a passing car caught his eye. Brandon was in the back seat, his forehead pressed against the window, his eyes closed. He looked worried.

Maddox frowned. Brandon should be at home recuperating. Why was he in town? And why did he look like something bad had happened? Maddox wished he could call his mate and ask what was happening, but he didn't have Brandon's number. Chances were that he was going to the police station, though, so instead of the coffee shop, Maddox headed there.

He got to the station parking lot just as Brandon was leaving the car. Maddox was still too far away to for Brandon to notice him—he wasn't about to start yelling in the middle of town and get everyone's attention—so he ran after Brandon, catching him and his parents in the station lobby. They were already talking with Patrick, and all of them looked like a disaster was about to happen, or already had.

The door slammed shut behind Maddox, making him wince, especially when half the people in the lobby turned to look. He swallowed and straightened his back. He was there for Brandon. No one cared about him.

The tension in Brandon's shoulders relaxed as Maddox walked closer, and Maddox knew he'd done the right thing. It didn't help him with putting his thoughts in order, but that could wait. Everything could wait if Brandon needed him. He hadn't quite realized that before, but he did now.

Maddox had always known about mates and how focused on each other they were, but it had never hit him the way it did now. Even though he and Brandon had only talked once, and about nothing important, even though he still wasn't sure he wanted to be with Brandon—or rather, if he'd be able to trust Brandon that way—he needed to be close to his mate. He needed to be there, to support Brandon through whatever was happening. It would make what came after awkward, but right now, that was the thing that mattered least.

"What's going on?" he asked as he got closer.

Patrick grimaced. "Maddox. I'm not sure—"

To Maddox's surprise, Brandon took his hand. He linked their fingers together and looked at Patrick, avoiding Maddox's gaze. "He's my mate. He can stay. He *needs* to stay and find out what happened."

Patrick rubbed his face. He looked like he'd had a rough day, and it made Maddox's chest tighten with anxiety. Something was wrong. "All right. Let's go to my office."

Brandon's mother didn't waste time. As soon as Patrick closed his office's door, she was on him. "What happened? How could you let that man escape? Hasn't my son been through enough already?"

Brandon sighed. "Mom. Stop freaking out and let him explain, yeah? We're not going to find out what's going on if you don't let him speak."

"Everyone sit down. Please," Patrick said.

Matt wasn't there today, but Maddox had no doubt he was on his way, especially now that he knew what had happened. Matt's presence in the hospital had made Maddox feel less like an outsider, less like he didn't belong in Brandon's family. They were similar, close but not part of it, especially Maddox.

"As you know from my phone call, Bart Miller, the man who drugged and assaulted Brandon, escaped this morning. He was being transferred to the council jail. He knocked out the Nix who was going to shimmer him there and ran."

"Why haven't you gotten him back?" Brandon's mom asked. She looked like she'd gladly go after the guy herself and possibly hand him back missing his balls. Maddox agreed with that sentiment.

"We've tried. Our Nix haven't been able to locate him, though, so he probably got his hands on one of the Nix neutralizers. You know how easy they are to find these days."

"Easy, maybe, but it's also expensive, especially the ones that are sold as jewelry, and I can't see the man going around town or even leaving town carrying one of the bulkier ones. Even in a car, it wouldn't be inconspicuous," Brandon's father pointed out.

He had a point. The first devices designed to block Nix and their powers had been huge. They still existed, but they were slowly being replaced by smaller items, things people could wear around their necks, or even on their fingers as rings. Those were expensive, though, and Bart hadn't had money on him when he'd escaped. How had he gotten his hands on one?

Patrick rubbed the back of his neck. "I dug into Bart Miller's past after we arrested him. He has ties with the Beasts."

Maddox's stomach dropped. The Beasts was a shifter gang that hated humans, but that didn't stop them from dealing drugs to them, and to shifters. They were behind the recent increase in overdoses and deaths in town, and Maddox hated them. Their drugs were killing people, humans and shifters alike, and while he hadn't noticed them personally, he knew they were there. None of his friends used, thank God, but he knew others did. "Was that why he was at the club?" he asked.

Patrick frowned. "What do you mean?"

"To deal drugs. I know the Beasts have their hands in other stuff, but that's the main reason they're here in Gillham, right? To deal drugs?"

"It is, and yes, we suspect that's why he was there last night."

"Who cares why he was at the club?" Brandon's mother snapped. "I want to know what you're doing to put him behind bars again. Is my son safe? Because we all heard that monster telling him he was going to kill him, and if something happens to my son, I'll hold you and the rest of the police force personally responsible."

Patrick raised his hands. "And I'll feel responsible. Trust me, this is the last thing I wanted to happen, and everyone here is doing whatever they can to get the guy. There's more at stake than just Brandon's safety. We need Bart Miller because he knows a lot about the Beasts and their business in town. Our goal is ultimately to get rid of them and their drugs. We've already had too many overdoses and deaths."

"Do you think he really is going to come for Brandon?" Brandon's dad asked.

Brandon had stayed silent through the entire conversation, and Maddox wasn't sure what to make of that. They were still holding hands, so he squeezed and forced himself to smile when Brandon looked at him.

Brandon didn't smile back.

Maddox wasn't surprised. There wasn't much to smile about in this situation.

"His record makes me think yes."

Maddox pulled his attention back to Patrick. He needed to hear this.

"Why?"

"Because he always goes after the people who slighted him. He's violent and vengeful."

Maddox didn't like this. "Wouldn't it be safer for him to leave town?" he asked.

"It would be, but the man isn't exactly rational. He

doesn't care about safety. I suspect he has faith the Beasts will keep him safe, even if he does end up behind bars. Brandon was the one who landed him in jail, though. The reason doesn't matter. We all saw how he reacted yesterday. I hope I'm wrong, but I wouldn't count on it. We can't afford to count on it."

"What are you going to do? Give Brandon protection?" Brandon's mother asked.

Patrick rubbed the back of his neck. "It would be better if Brandon left town for a bit."

"No." That was Brandon. It was the first time he said anything, and Maddox held his breath. "I know you all want to keep me safe, but I'm not running. There's no way to know if or when Bart Miller is going to be caught. I could be away for months, and I don't want that. Gillham is my home, and I'm not leaving."

Patrick pressed his lips together. "I understand that. But you can't stay at home. It's too dangerous."

"What about my dad's place?"

"If Bart Miller knows where you live, he'll know where your father lives, too."

"What about my place?" Maddox said before he could think better of it.

Everyone looked at him. "Your place?" Patrick asked.

"Brandon is my mate, but it's not common knowledge. We only met yesterday. We'd never had contact before, so I doubt anyone is going to make the connection."

Brandon's dad leaned forward. "You're offering your house as a safe place for Brandon to live until this is over?"

Maddox knew he was going to regret it. Hell, he already did. But Brandon was his mate, and even if he weren't, he was in danger. Maddox couldn't ignore that, not when there was something he could do to help. "Yes."

CHAPTER FOUR

Brandon could tell Maddox already regretted offering to let him move in with him. Even though it would only be until Bart Miller was caught—there was no way Brandon's mother would let him stay one second longer than necessary, even with Maddox being his mate, or maybe especially because of that—it had a heavy meaning. Brandon didn't expect anything to happen between them, but he hoped it would. He'd noticed how wary Maddox seemed, though, so he wouldn't hope too much, or at least, he'd try not to.

"Matt and I will drive you and Brandon back," Brandon's dad told Maddox as they walked into to house where Brandon still lived. Jason was home, and music came from his room. It was going to be weird for Brandon not to share the house with his brother.

Shit. He hadn't thought much about it yet, but he was going to live with Maddox. He'd never lived with anyone but his family. What if Maddox hated the way he ate, or that he snored when he had a cold? Not that they were going to share a bed or even a room. Maddox had explained Brandon was welcome to his guest room, and even though Brandon felt kind of sorry about that, he was also relieved. He didn't know how he'd have behaved if he'd had to share a bed with his mate. He wasn't a virgin, but all the guys he'd been with had been hookups, nothing as serious as a mate. Of course, there was little in life as serious as mates.

"Thank you, Sir."

Brandon's dad scowled. "I told you to call me Colin. And

it's the least we can do since we forced your hand."

"You didn't. I offered my house, and I stand by it. Brandon will be safe with me."

"I know."

Brandon's mother huffed and went upstairs. "I'm going to put together the clothes you still have in the laundry room," she said without looking back.

Brandon knew she was worried, but he was also aware of the fact that she didn't like him living with Maddox. They were mates, but in her eyes, Brandon was too young to be thinking about mating.

And she wasn't wrong. Brandon knew he and Maddox would eventually bond, or at least he hoped so, but he wasn't ready. He didn't know Maddox, and with Bart Miller hounding him, there was no way he wanted to make that big a step. Besides, it didn't look like Maddox was any more ready than he was, even though he was ten years older.

Brandon's father patted his shoulder. "Why don't you and Maddox go up to your room? Don't pack too much stuff. You can call if you need more."

"Patrick said not to visit me too often," Brandon pointed out. Having his parents coming and going from Maddox's house would reveal that was where he was staying as surely as if he stood on the porch and waved at Miller.

"I know, but it doesn't mean we can't meet with Maddox and give him whatever you need. We'll find a way, don't worry. So take only the things you can't do without."

Brandon wondered if that included his school books. Probably, knowing his parents. His mom had already told him she'd talk to the principal on Monday, but since the principal was a pack member, having Brandon skip school wouldn't be a problem. He'd have trouble if he didn't study at all until he went back, though.

He bit his lower lip and looked at Maddox. "Do you want

to come help me?" Brandon mostly wanted to be able to talk to his mate alone, at least for a moment.

Maddox looked at the front door as if he was considering running out, but instead of doing that, he nodded. "Of course. I'll help you carry your bags to the car."

They climbed the stairs in silence, and Brandon frantically tried to remember if he'd made his bed this morning and if he'd put his dirty clothes into the hamper. His mom always told him to, but he'd been dead tired last night when he'd come home from the hospital, and he hadn't thought much beyond getting his ass into bed.

Luckily for him, there was no dirty laundry on the floor, although his bed wasn't made. He rushed to it and pulled the sheets up. His mom would no doubt change them once he was gone, but he didn't want Maddox to think he was a slob, even though he was a bit. "You can sit on the bed, or at the desk if you'd rather have a chair," he said. He knew he was babbling, but he wasn't sure how to stop himself.

Maddox perched on the edge of the chair at the desk, and Brandon got to work. He didn't need many clothes. He wasn't allowed to leave Maddox's house as long as Bart Miller was out there, so he picked mostly sweats and jeans, things he'd be comfortable in. He added t-shirts and sweaters, his heart beating faster when he had to open his underwear drawer, but Maddox wasn't even looking at him.

Brandon sighed. "I can find another place, you know."

Maddox's head snapped toward him. Maybe he'd been lost in his thoughts rather than ignoring Brandon. Brandon wasn't sure how he could do either. He hadn't been able to stop thinking about Maddox since they'd met. He was *supposed* to. They were mates, even though they were young and not ready for anything close to bonding.

"What do you mean?"

Brandon took a deep breath and turned to face Maddox.

"I know you offered your house, but it's obvious you don't want me there. If the only reason you do is that you feel obligated because we're mates, it's okay, but I don't want you to be uncomfortable because of me. I mean, you live alone, right?"

Maddox nodded

Brandon went on, "There's a reason you live alone. Maybe you don't like people, or maybe you don't like me, I don't know. But you don't have to force yourself. I'm sure Kameron can find me another place to stay. Hell, I can probably stay with him and Zach."

"No. I offered, and I won't change my mind."

"I get that, but you don't have to, not if you don't want me there. I'd hate to—to inconvenience you." Brandon hated saying those words to his mate, but he had to.

Maddox got up. Brandon pressed closer to the dresser, unsure what to expect. Maddox might have saved him from being raped, but they didn't know each other. Brandon doubted he was violent because Kameron wouldn't have let him stay with the pack, but still.

Maddox stopped in front of Brandon and looked him in the eyes. "You're not a bother. I won't kick you out. You're welcome at my house for as long as you want or need. I'm going to go there right now and make sure everything is ready for you, okay?"

"You don't have to."

Maddox smiled, and God, it was glorious. Brandon didn't think he'd seen him smile yet, not a real smile like this one. "I know, but you weren't exactly comfortable when I walked in here, right? The same goes for me. I'm just going to check the guest room is clean and that there's no cat puke anywhere."

Brandon smiled back. "You have a cat?"

Maddox laughed, shocking Brandon again. "I do. I hope

you like animals, because I have several."

"I love animals. The only reason I don't have a pet is that my mom never wanted one."

"You'll have your fill of pets living with me, don't worry. See you in a few, Brandon."

Brandon watched Maddox leave his bedroom. His gaze wandered down to Maddox's ass, and he didn't bother trying to look away because damn, that was a fine ass.

He had to force himself to get back to packing, but once he did, it didn't take him long to grab everything he needed and carry it downstairs. His mom was hovering by the front door, and she made a beeline for him, slamming against him and wrapping her arms around his waist. Brandon hugged back. He and his mom might not always get along, but they loved each other, and he knew how worried she was. "I'll be okay," he murmured, hoping he wasn't lying.

"I know. You can't leave the house. And I put some pepper spray in that bag, just in case you need to keep Maddox away."

"*Maddox?* Mom, he's not the one I need to be afraid of."

She pushed away and looked up at him. "I know. But he's a man, and he's ten years older than you. He'll want . . . things from you, and I want you to know you can say no."

Brandon was pretty sure she was talking about sex, and the last thing he wanted was to have that conversation again, especially with Maddox in the mix. "I know, Mom."

"Leave him be, Justine," Brandon's dad said as he walked in. "Maddox is a good man. He won't force Brandon to do anything he doesn't want." He looked at Brandon. "Ready?"

Brandon wasn't sure he'd ever be, not for something like this, but he nodded anyway.

Maddox looked around his living room. There wasn't much

else he could do to make the place acceptable to someone else. He'd vacuumed the floors and the couch, then he'd cleaned the paw prints from the coffee table. He'd made sure the dogs and cats were clean and that Fritz's cage wasn't too nasty. The litter boxes were in the laundry room, and he'd emptied them this morning, so they were okay.

It was too late to do anything else, though, because Maddox could hear a car parking in front of his house. He peeked around the curtain and swallowed at the sight of his mate getting out of his father's car. Matt tried to grab a bag, but Colin shook his head, and Maddox remembered Matt had been wounded not too long ago. He didn't use a cane to walk anymore, but he still limped. The small gesture Colin had done for his mate made Maddox's heart ache. Would things be like that between him and Brandon?

Maddox shook that thought away. He couldn't start thinking about a hypothetical future between himself and Brandon, not right now. Maybe later, once Brandon was safe and he didn't *have* to rely on Maddox. But at the moment, he did, and Maddox wasn't going to take anything he did or said seriously, not when it came to the bond between them. Brandon was vulnerable and scared, and that was enough to confuse him and his feelings.

Maddox went to open the door. He'd crated the dogs so they wouldn't run out and had made sure the cats were all in the laundry room. They did leave the house sometimes, but Maddox knew he wouldn't be in the mood to search the woods for them tonight, so it was better if they stayed in at least today. Besides, they'd soon be busy examining Brandon and his things. That ought to distract them — and Brandon.

Brandon was looking around when Maddox opened the door, and he smiled at him. It was lighter and happier than when he'd smiled before, and Maddox hoped that meant he liked the house. He was aware of the fact that most people preferred to live closer to the center of the pack and the other houses, but he'd picked this isolated spot on purpose. He'd always been a loner, and that hadn't changed when he'd decided to move out of his adoptive family's house to be on his own. He seldom saw people unless he went to work or actively looked for them, or of course unless they decided to do an intervention like Asher had last night. That didn't happen often, thank God, so Brandon would be safe here.

"Thanks again for this," Colin said as he joined Brandon on the porch. They waited for Matt, then Maddox led the way inside.

"There's no need to thank me. I know this place isn't much, but it's all I need."

"Not much? It's great," Brandon said, and he sounded like he meant it.

There wasn't much to the house, though. Maddox had taken advantage of the pack's generosity when Kameron had offered to pay for the house like he had with almost everyone else in the pack. He'd made sure he'd have more than enough space for the future, so there were three bedrooms, each of them with their own bathroom, a wide kitchen, a comfortable living room, and even a garage with a laundry room that was big enough to contain his dogs' crates. Maddox didn't need an office or anything like that, so the bedrooms were reserved for guests, but Brandon was the first guest he'd ever had. Asher had slept over a few times, but he was Maddox's best friend, so he didn't count, not from Maddox's point of view.

Colin helped Brandon carry his things to the second floor. Maddox expected him and Matt to hang around for a bit, so he was surprised when Colin hugged Brandon and said, "We better go."

"I promise to call if anything happens," Brandon said.

His father glared. "No, you promise to call every day so

your mother and I will know you're safe."

"And if something happens. Got it, Dad. Don't worry. I'm safe here."

"I know. I wouldn't have agreed to this otherwise."

Maddox wasn't sure why everyone seemed to have so much faith in him, but he wasn't about to ask.

Someone in the laundry room barked, and everyone's head whipped that way. Brandon bounced on his feet. "Can I go see?"

"You can let them out if you want. They're in the laundry room, off the kitchen." He hesitated. "Don't be afraid of any of them."

"*Any* of them?"

"Yes. I . . . have a lot of pets. But they're all well behaved, and none of them bite. Well, except Queen Elizabeth, but only when she wants me to feed her, and never hard enough to draw blood."

Brandon's eyes widened. "Queen Elizabeth? Oh, I need to see her." He hugged his father, then Matt. "I'll be here if you need me. Bye!"

Then he was gone, leaving Matt, Colin, and Maddox blinking after him. Colin cleared his throat and faced Maddox. "You have Patrick's number?"

"Of course. And yours. And your ex-wife's. And Matt's."

Colin smiled deprecatingly. "Yes, well. He's my son. I'm allowed to be worried."

"I never said anything otherwise."

"Kameron said he'd have the guards patrol in this area of pack territory more often, but not often enough that it's obvious. You have to call him if you notice anything strange."

"I know." Kameron had called Maddox only minutes after Maddox had arrived home earlier. He and Patrick were working together to make sure Brandon was safe, and Maddox was glad. No matter how much faith Brandon and everyone else seem to have in him, he felt better knowing he had back-up.

Brandon was sitting on the floor in the laundry room when Maddox got there after seeing Colin and Matt out. He was laughing, his hands buried in Madame Mimsy's fur while Colonel Bau tried to climb into his lap. Queen Elizabeth watched him from the counter, her eyes narrowed, but the other three cats and dog were all vying for Brandon's attention. Maddox had the absurd urge to shift and take Colonel Bau's place in Brandon's lap, but he stayed human. "Everything okay in here?" he asked.

Brandon was still smiling widely when he looked up at Maddox. His cheeks were flushed, and his eyes glittered. All the worry he'd been carrying since yesterday was gone, at least for a moment, and Maddox's caracal felt smug that they had been the ones to do that. Maddox thought it was the animals rather than him, but did it matter? His house seemed to be a haven of peace for Brandon already, and that was the only thing he cared about. He wasn't sure how he'd deal with having to share his space with someone else, but he was about to find out.

"They're great, and you have so many."

Maddox shrugged. "I work at the shelter. I usually end up taking home the animals who don't find their forever home."

Brandon's smile softened. "That's very good of you. Did you only take cats and dogs?"

"No. I have two rabbits outside and a parrot in the living room." He rubbed the back of his neck. "So, I was wondering what you wanted to eat for dinner? Someone is going to bring me my car, and I bought some groceries earlier, but I didn't know you were going to live with me, so I only bought enough for me."

Brandon gently pushed Colonel Bau off his lap and got

up. He brushed his ass, and Maddox wanted to volunteer to do it for him, or maybe to check if it was clean. He kept his gaze focused firmly on Brandon's face, though. "I don't care what we eat, honestly. I'm not hungry yet, but I guess that might change. What did you have in mind? Maybe I can help cook."

"You cook?" Maddox was surprised. He'd thought that since Brandon still lived at home, his mother did the cooking.

"Somewhat. Don't ask my mom about the cookies I tried to make last year, though. She hasn't been able to get the soot stains out of the kitchen walls yet."

Maddox blinked. "You set fire to the kitchen?"

"No! I got distracted, that's all. I'm sure the cookies would have been delicious. I just forgot to take them out."

Maddox wasn't sure what to think of that, but he wasn't going to say no to the help Brandon offered. If they were going to live together, they needed to learn what they could or couldn't do and to find a way to divide the tasks.

Brandon kept sneaking glances at Maddox, so he knew his mate was uncomfortable. He wasn't sure if it was because he suddenly had to share his house or if Brandon, in particular, was making him feel that way, but he wished he knew how to fix it. He'd already suggested he could find another place to stay and Maddox had said no. He wasn't going to offer again—he wanted to stay with Maddox and to get to know him, and he felt safe with him. What could he do, though?

Maddox stirred the vegetables in the pan. "This should be done. I hope it's good."

"I'm sure it is," Brandon said quietly.

"I'm not used to cooking for other people."

Was that it? Was Maddox uncomfortable because he

wanted to make a good impression? It made sense in a way. No matter how little he wanted Brandon there, they were still mates. "You don't have to do anything special for me, you know?"

Maddox looked up. He was frowning, and Brandon wanted to soothe the expression out. "I'm not. It's just stir fry."

Brandon smiled. "I didn't mean just for the food. I eat pretty much anything, so that's not a problem. But it's obvious you don't know how to behave with me around, so I wanted you to know I don't need anything special." Brandon bit his lower lip. "And I don't expect anything from you in any way." He hadn't been sure how to bring that up, but this was a good time. Okay, maybe not a *good* one, but Brandon doubted there would actually be one, in any conversation.

"What do you mean?"

Brandon groaned. Of course he'd have to explain. "I mean because we're mates. I know it's a weird situation and everything. We don't know each other, but we're going to have to live together for a while. We haven't had the chance to talk about anything other than the guy after me." Brandon didn't want to do this, but they needed to clear the air. "If you don't want to be with me, if you don't want us to bond, or even to have a relationship, that's fine."

Maddox put the wooden spoon down and turned toward Brandon. "It is?"

Yeah, Brandon *definitely* didn't want to do this. "Yes. I mean, I know not everyone ends up with their mate, and not only because they died or whatever. Sometimes things don't work out, and it's pretty obvious you're keeping your distance. I guess what I'm trying to say is that it's okay to be disappointed that I'm your mate. I'm only eighteen, I'm still in high school, and I went and did something stupid like letting someone drug me and drag me into a bathroom."

"You didn't do anything wrong, Brandon. You might not have been as careful as you should have, but that bottle of water was sealed when you got it, and like you said, Bart Miller only had it for a few seconds. It's obvious he knew what he was doing, and I doubt it was his first time. And who said I was disappointed?"

Brandon shrugged. "No one. You just look like you're not sure what to do with me." Brandon blushed. He hadn't meant to say that the way it sounded. "You know what I mean."

Maddox shuffled. "I do. And honestly, I don't. I told you I don't have a lot of people in my life. That's because I don't like a lot of people. I'm fine by myself."

Brandon's heart sank. "I see."

Maddox huffed. "That's not what I meant."

"It's okay, though. I get it."

Brandon needed some time. He had to get over this stupid heartache. He was going to stay with Maddox for some time, and he didn't want to be like a heartbroken puppy following his master around. Not that Maddox was his master. No, he was his mate, and even though he didn't want him, it meant something. Brandon wasn't sure what, but he'd find out.

He forced himself to smile. "You know what? I'm not hungry. I'm just going to go to bed, if that's okay with you. I had a hard day, and yesterday, well, you know how that went. Thanks for cooking, though, and if you don't mind leaving everything in the sink, I'll wash the dishes tomorrow morning."

Brandon knew he should talk this out with Maddox like an adult, but he *wasn't* an adult. He was just a kid, and he didn't need Maddox to point that out. He knew it. The way his mom treated him meant she didn't trust him, and how could she after what had happened last night? Brandon had been angry at her for suggesting it had been his fault, but it kind of had. If he hadn't taken his eyes off the bottle of water, or if he'd thrown it away instead of drinking it, he wouldn't have been drugged and everything else.

And he probably wouldn't have met Maddox.

He wasn't sure if that would have been a good thing or a bad one, and he doubted he'd find out soon. He and his wolf were over the moon at having found his mate, although he was more cautious than the wolf because he knew how complicated human emotions were. He was the first one conflicted about this, and he hadn't expected Maddox to want to bond right away or anything, but their conversation had felt like a rejection.

He could handle it if it was.

Probably.

No, he *could* handle it and be nice to Maddox. He just needed a moment to wrap his mind around everything. Tomorrow morning he'd be through with it, and he'd be able to see this was the best thing to do. Maddox was used to being on his own. He didn't want a mate or a boyfriend. He'd probably have one if he did. He was nice enough, and God knew he was gorgeous. Anyone with eyes would see that. Then there were his pets. He had a soft spot for animals and apparently brought home the strays that didn't find a home, and Brandon found that endearing and adorable.

Maddox didn't ask him to wait or to talk. He didn't ask anything. He didn't make a sound as Brandon left the kitchen, followed by one of the dogs. All of the dogs and cats had a tag with their name at the collar, but Brandon couldn't remember some of them.

He climbed the stairs and went to his bedroom. He left the door slightly open in case the dogs or the cats were used to sleeping in the room during the night and flopped onto the bed. He'd left his phone on the nightstand earlier because he thought he and Maddox would talk and he hadn't wanted to be disturbed. He took it and brought the screen to life, smiling when he saw messages in the group text he had going on with Nathalie and Lee.

Brandon???

Leave him alone, Lee. He's probably busy unpacking.

Or making out with his mate. Lee had added a winking emoji that made Brandon smile. He wished he was making out with Maddox.

Something jumped onto the bed, and Brandon turned to see who it was. He peered at the tag on the dog's neck and smiled at the name. "Hey. Princess Pawpington. Can I call you Princess? Your name is a mouthful, you know."

She didn't answer, of course, but she settled down against his side. He rubbed her neck and went back to his phone. He quickly typed, *well, I am in bed with a beast, but not Maddox unfortunately.*

It took Lee only a handful of seconds to answer. *What do you mean??? Pics!*

Brandon hugged Princess and took a selfie. She licked his cheek just as he snapped, and when he checked the picture, he looked happy, happier than he felt. He sent it anyway. He'd talk with Lee and Nathalie eventually, and he'd tell them how much it hurt, but not now. They'd worry and want to come over, and Brandon didn't think that was a good idea.

Beautiful! Lee answered.

Her name is Princess Pawpington. Lee would get a kick out of that.

I bet she's not too happy about that name.

I don't know. She looks okay.

Of course she does. She's with you. I wish I could come over.

Brandon sent a crying emoji, then, *I wish so too. But this is safer.*

I know. As long as you tell me everything that happens with Maddox. And by everything, I mean everything. There was another winking emoji after that, along with a peach one, and an eggplant one.

Brandon laughed. Yes, he was sad about what was happening with Maddox, but he'd always have his friends and his family, and that would be enough.

Maddox ate a piece of carrot, chewed, and swallowed. It might as well have been dust because he didn't taste it.

He sighed and put his fork down, then looked at the door. It was open—it always was. Open doors were a must when you had so many animals moving around the house—but there were no signs of Brandon. Maddox wasn't sure where he'd gone wrong earlier, no matter how much he thought about it.

He'd told Brandon that what had happened wasn't his fault. He'd told him he wasn't disappointed about having him as a mate. He'd tried to explain that the reason he was so awkward was that he wasn't used to being around people, but for some reason, Brandon had been offended by that.

Or at least Maddox thought he'd been offended. He wasn't sure, because he hadn't gone after Brandon. He knew he should talk to him and explain himself better, but he wasn't sure he could. That was why he felt better with animals than with humans. His animals didn't get offended when he said something stupid, and they'd never leave him. They loved him. They also wouldn't kick him out of his house because they hated him and what he was.

Maddox sighed again. He didn't know what to do, and that meant he needed help. He didn't want to call Asher, though, because Asher would want to come over to talk and shit, and that was the last thing Maddox wanted. Couldn't anyone do this kind of stuff through texts or a phone call? He'd rather text, but a call would be faster, and he felt he needed to clear things out with Brandon before they went to sleep.

He decided to text Gabriel. He was quieter than Asher and didn't stick his nose into anyone's business, but he didn't miss much. He'd no doubt know what was going on already. *I messed up with Brandon. How do I fix it?*

He didn't wait for an answer. He got up and cleaned up—no matter what Brandon had said, Maddox wasn't going to leave everything out for him—then made sure the animals had water. He grabbed his phone on his way outside with two of the three dogs. The house had a fenced yard, so he sat on the porch as he let them run around and sniff to their hearts' content.

Gabriel had answered. *What did you do?*

I'm not sure. I told him I wasn't disappointed but that I was better alone.

Maddox didn't like the three dots that appeared when someone was typing a message. He couldn't help but stare at them and wonder, especially because it took Gabriel a while to get his answer together.

So basically you told him you don't want him in your life.

Of course not!

Sure looks like it if that's really what you told him.

It's not what I meant, though.

Then you need to be clearer. You're awkward with people on your best days, and he's traumatized by what happened to him. You have to put everything out there and make sure there's no misunderstanding between the two of you.

Maddox hated talking, especially about feelings. It looked like he was going to have to, though. He wasn't looking forward to it, but it was unavoidable, and Gabriel was right—Brandon was traumatized, and he didn't need Maddox messing his life up even more by not being honest with him.

Thanks.

You're welcome. And don't mess this up. He might be young, and you might not like people, but he's not someone you can brush off. He's your mate, and you'll only ever have one of those.

Maddox had also only had one set of parents, and look how that had ended up. He didn't tell Gabriel, of course, but just like Asher, his friend knew him.

Mates are chosen for you. Your parents shouldn't have had kids if they weren't ready to accept them for who they were. Besides, you found a new family, didn't you? He's not your parents, and he won't reject you. I'm pretty sure he knows you're gay, and really, if there's one person who can accept all of you, it's your mate.

Maddox put his phone in his pocket. Maybe Gabriel was right. Maddox's parents hadn't thought anything of kicking him out of the house because he liked boys, but Brandon wasn't them. For one, he knew Maddox was gay, and he was probably gay himself. Did his parents know, though? It would be hypocritical of Colin not to support his son, but Maddox wouldn't find it surprising. Colin didn't seem to care, and from the little Maddox had seen of him, he was a good man who was ready to support his son through whatever happened to him and whatever he wanted. Brandon's mom seemed different. But Maddox hadn't had enough contact with her to be sure.

Besides, Brandon wasn't Maddox's parents, but he wasn't *his* parents either, so what his mom thought of Maddox or of being gay didn't matter.

And Maddox shouldn't assume without talking to Brandon. It wasn't fair, to either of them. He didn't want to grovel, but he was going to have to. He hated the thought of Brandon thinking he wasn't good enough when he was everything Maddox could want from a mate. He was young, yes, but that wouldn't matter in even five years. But the rest was perfect. He loved his parents and his brother, he had a good head on his shoulders, he cared about school, he had friends. Maddox was going to find out more about him as the time passed, but for now, he had no problem with what he saw, and he knew himself well enough to realize the problem was his, not Brandon's. He was the one who was terrified Brandon might realize he could have better, or that something was wrong with Maddox and Brandon couldn't stand it.

Maddox shook his head. He had to stop thinking this way, because it would taint whatever relationship he and Brandon might have.

He got up and whistled for the dogs. Princess Pawpington had never come down, but he wasn't surprised. She preferred her bed to the great outdoors. She'd only go out to do her business and go right back inside. He was going to take them out again later anyway. He'd make sure she was there before he crated the dogs for the night. Madame Mimsy wasn't eager to go back inside, but she agreed when Maddox waved a treat in front of her nose. He made sure all the animals were okay, then grabbed a pint of ice cream and two spoons before going upstairs.

He expected Brandon's door to be closed, but it wasn't, and the opening was enough for Maddox to be able to see the bed. He felt a bit like a creep, but the sight was adorable. Brandon was lying on his side, his eyes closed, Princess Pawpington curled against his chest. He was hugging her as if she were a stuffed animal, and she didn't seem to mind.

Lord Nibbles had also found his way into the bedroom, and he'd taken post on the pillow around Brandon's head. Maddox could hear him purr even from where he was, and he didn't want to interrupt or wake Brandon up. He'd hoped they could clear things up before going to bed, but he was too late.

He turned to leave. The floor creaked under his foot, and

Brandon's eyes flew open. There was a bit of panic in his gaze, but it lasted for barely more than a second. Then he relaxed and smiled. "Did you need something?" he asked without sitting up.

Maddox held up the pint of ice cream. "I was wondering if we could talk?"

"And you brought ice cream? Are you planning to break my heart?"

"Of course not. I was trying to do something nice. I'm not used to this, though, so I'm sorry if I messed up."

Brandon sat up. Lord Nibbles glared at him, but he didn't move from the pillow, curling on himself and closing his eyes. Brandon patted the mattress next to him, and Maddox sat beside him. He held out one of the spoons and opened the pint, offering it to Brandon first.

What now? He cleared his throat. "I'm sorry if I made you think you weren't good enough, because you are. What I meant to say when I told you I'm used to being alone is just that. I don't have many friends. I don't have a family, not a blood family anyway. My parents kicked me out when I was fifteen when I came out to them. I still carry that around, even though I know it's wrong. I just keep expecting you to realize you can find better or that I'm wrong for you and leave. I wouldn't blame you." Because if his parents had, how could anyone else not?

"Oh, Maddox. I'm sorry that happened to you. But I'm not planning on leaving."

"Not right now. You can't."

Brandon shook his head. "Not ever, not for as long as you'll have me. I'd offer to bond so you can be sure of that, but I'm not ready for that."

"Neither am I."

Brandon sucked on his spoon. "But I also don't want to go through this again. Can we agree to be honest with each other from now on? To say what's on our minds without hiding anything even if we think it's best? I hate feeling like you don't want me."

How could Maddox tell Brandon he wasn't sure he did? That even though Brandon was enough, he didn't think *he* was?

CHAPTER FIVE

Brandon glared at the TV. Would it really kill Maddox to talk to him? He'd thought they'd been making progress when Maddox had come to his room with ice cream a few days ago, but they'd barely talked since then, and not because he didn't want to.

Hadn't they gone over this? Maddox was used to being on his own, but he wasn't on his own anymore. Brandon was there with him, and while he understood it would take some time for both of them to get used to it, it wouldn't happen if Maddox hid in his room or left the house with the dogs every time Brandon tried talking to him.

The truth was, Brandon was lonely. He'd never been one of those people who had hundreds of friends, but he'd also never been alone. He usually had his mom and his brother around, and he saw Lee and Nathalie almost every day. They went to school together, and they usually spent weekends together, too, sometimes all three of them, sometimes just two of them. Brandon hadn't seen anyone but Maddox in three days, though, and he was going crazy.

It was time for him to invite his best friends over.

Maddox had told him he didn't have a problem with that, and while they'd need to be careful, they were part of the small group of people Brandon trusted. There was no way they'd tell anyone where he was, and Bart Miller hadn't been seen since he'd escaped. Brandon was pretty sure he'd left town, and even if he hadn't, Brandon was in pack territory. There was no way Bart could get to him, even if he tried.

Kameron would make sure of that. Him staying with Maddox was just a precaution, one he'd been happy to take when he'd thought it would bring him and Maddox closer.

It hadn't, and now he was lonely.

He took out his phone and called Nathalie since he knew Lee was helping his dad with something and wouldn't be able to answer. Even though he was busy, he'd come over later if Brandon asked him to. He'd been wanting to come since day one, and Brandon had hated telling him no.

"What's up?" Nathalie answered.

"I'm bored." Brandon knew he was whining, but he didn't care. She was one of his best friends. She was used to him whining and generally making a nuisance of himself.

She tsked. "Of course you are. You're stuck in a house. Ask your mate to distract you."

"He won't even talk to me, Nat. Can you and Lee come? Please?"

Nathalie didn't answer right away. Brandon frowned, wondering if something was wrong until she asked, "Are you sure it's a good idea?"

"Why wouldn't it be?"

"Because you're supposed to be hiding, Bran. Having Lee and me there will make it pretty obvious it's where you're hiding."

Trust Nathalie to be more serious about this than Brandon was. "I know, but come on. We're in pack territory, and we both know there's no way Bart can come in here. Having me stay with Maddox is just a precaution. I'd have been fine with my mother or my father as long as I don't leave pack territory, and I'm not about to. Besides, neither Kameron nor Patrick said anything about me not having people over. They said to be careful and not to do it every day, but I haven't seen you and Lee in a week."

Nathalie snorted. "More like three days, but okay. I miss

you, and I know Lee does, too."

"Then come."

"Won't your mate mind?"

He probably would, but he'd told Brandon he could invite his friends. Besides, Brandon wouldn't have had to if Maddox would only talk to him. He wouldn't be lonely then. "Nope. He said I could have people over. He's been ignoring me and spending most of his time away, so he probably won't even notice."

"That doesn't sound good."

"It's not." Not for Brandon's soft heart anyway.

"I'll grab Lee on my way over. Give us twenty minutes."

Brandon smiled as he hung up. He was looking forward to catching up with his friends. They called each other and texted every day, but it wasn't the same.

He got up and went to look for Maddox to tell him his friends were coming over. Maddox might have said it was okay with him, but Brandon didn't want him to be surprised and freak out when he walked into his living room and found three people there instead of just him. Maddox wasn't anywhere to be found, though. He wasn't in the kitchen or in his bedroom, where a pile of cats were sleeping on the bed. The dogs were around the house, so he hadn't taken them out. He usually told Brandon when he left the house, so it was strange that he hadn't this time, but Brandon didn't think much of it once Lee and Nathalie got there.

Lee looked around curiously, while Nathalie's expression was a little lost. Brandon hugged her and noticed she'd gotten thinner. He wasn't going to bring it up because it just wasn't something they usually talked about, but she was already thin, and losing more weight was going to make her disappear. Maybe he could ask Lee about it, although he suspected it was the stress of what was happening to him. He might be the one in the middle of it, but Lee and Nathalie were his best friends, so they weren't far away.

"It's nice," Lee declared as they sat on the couch.

"It is. And Maddox is great, too."

Lee arched a brow. "Are you sure? Because from what Nat told me, you didn't sound thrilled with him on the phone."

Brandon sighed. "He's just so remote, you know? He told me he was used to living alone and not seeing anyone often, but I thought he just meant he was kind of a loner. And he is, just much more than I thought."

"What do you mean?"

Brandon didn't want to give away Maddox's secrets, but he trusted his friends. "I think something bad happened to him in the past. I don't know much about him, but he wasn't born in the pack. Whatever did happen is still influencing him, I guess. He keeps everyone at arm's length, including me."

Nathalie frowned. "But you're his mate. You'll never hurt him."

"I know that, and he probably does, too, but it's hard to believe stuff sometimes, even though you know it's true."

"So he's ignoring you?" Lee asked. He looked like he was about to go find Maddox and drag him to Brandon, maybe even tie him up so he couldn't leave again.

Brandon's chest warmed. It might not have been the smartest thing to do, but he was glad he'd called his friends. "Yeah. We see each other at meals, and he talks to me, so it's not a total ignoring, but he spends a lot of time on his own, more than I wish he did. I thought that me living here with him would mean we'd get to know each other and maybe even get together, but so far, I've spent more time alone than with him." Brandon didn't want to think that maybe Maddox didn't like what he saw and heard when they were together, not after Maddox had reassured him, but he couldn't help it, not when Maddox was putting a lot of effort into not spending time with him.

"You need to talk to him and make things clear," Lee declared. "Whatever happened to him, you didn't do anything, and it's not fair that he won't give you a chance to show him you're a good guy."

Brandon looked at Nathalie, not surprised when she had a different opinion. "You should give him time. I agree that he should give you a chance, but he doesn't know you."

"He won't get to know Brandon if he doesn't spend time with him, though," Lee pointed out.

"But forcing him to talk won't help, either. He's probably trying to work things out without hurting Brandon."

Brandon could believe that, but he'd waited long enough. He didn't expect Maddox to want to bond with him or anything, but they could at least talk. He didn't even want to talk about them or their non-existent relationship. He'd be okay with watching a movie with Maddox or maybe talk about some of the books Maddox always seemed to be reading. Anything to reach out to his mate and feel less like he'd been a disappointment.

But when he went to look for Maddox once Lee and Nathalie had left, he still couldn't find him. He went back to Maddox's room, not seeing him there, but something on the bed caught his eyes. He knew the animals who lived in the house by now, and he was sure that the sand colored cat with the long black-tipped ears sleeping curled against Prince Whiskerton wasn't one of Maddox's. He couldn't have adopted a new pet since he hadn't left the house, so Brandon crept closer to get a better look.

The cat was an exotic one, he was sure of it, and since Maddox was a cat shifter—a caracal cat shifter—he was pretty sure who he was looking at.

God, it was adorable. Maddox was half buried under

Prince Whiskerton, and he didn't stir when Brandon gently touched the top of his head.

Brandon sat cross-legged on the floor by the bed and rested his chin on the mattress to get a better look. He wasn't going to wake Maddox up, but he wanted to, so much.

"I wish you were easier to get through to," Brandon said.

Maddox knew he shouldn't be listening to this. Brandon thought he was sleeping, and Maddox should show him he wasn't. He could simply move or open his eyes. But the pain in Brandon's voice stopped him. He knew he wasn't easy to live with, and he'd given Brandon space, thinking he was doing the right thing. They'd talked, and he'd been clear about the fact that he wasn't used to living with anyone, but he hadn't realized he was hurting his mate.

"I mean, you were clear when we talked the other day, and I understand you're used to being alone. I guess I thought I'd be different. I'm your mate. I *should* be different."

And he was. No matter how much space Maddox had given Brandon, he was always aware of him, of where he was in the house, and most times, of what he was doing. He felt a bit like a stalker, which was one of the reasons he'd forced himself to stay away. He'd thought Brandon would come to him if he wanted company, but now that he'd relaxed, he was realizing maybe Brandon had been doing the same thing, giving him space after their conversation and waiting for him to take the first step.

Maddox was an idiot.

He still wasn't sure what he wanted from Brandon or what he was ready for, but he didn't want to hurt his mate. He just wasn't sure how not to do it.

It had taken meeting his mate to realize how isolated he

was, and that it was his own fault. He'd known he kept everyone away, of course, but he'd thought he wanted it. And he did, but only up to a point. He could easily imagine what would happen if he didn't let Brandon in, and he didn't like it.

Maddox enjoyed being alone, but he didn't like being lonely, and sometimes, he did feel that way. The only way to solve that was to reach out, and he did so with selected people — Asher, Alice, Gabriel. Brandon wanted to qualify for that select group — he wanted to be one of the people Maddox trusted enough to let him into his life and his heart, and for the first time in his life, Maddox wanted it, too.

He'd always kept people away, even people who wanted to break through his hard shell. The family who'd adopted him loved him, but they'd stopped reaching out and waited for him to do it. The only one who pushed even when Maddox hated him for it was Asher.

Brandon wasn't as forceful. He was more like Gabriel, who seemed happy to leave Maddox to his brooding until he was ready for it to be over. Or at least that was what Maddox had thought, but it was obvious he'd been wrong. Brandon was hurt by the distance between them. He wanted them to breach it, to eliminate it, and Maddox wanted to do that for him.

Because no matter what, Brandon was his mate, and it *did* mean something. Maddox might have tried to convince himself otherwise, but he knew he was wrong. He'd known since the beginning.

Brandon was his mate. That meant that he was the one person who would probably stay with him for the rest of his life. He *could* leave, just like Maddox could if he wanted to, but they'd both be miserable. Even if they never bonded, their animals would always try to pull them toward each other. They didn't care about abandonment issues or fear.

They wanted their mate. The only way to make them stop would be for either Maddox or Brandon to leave Gillham, and neither of them would. Brandon didn't seem to want to, and Maddox wasn't sure he could completely give up on the chance to be loved.

He knew he was by other people. Asher loved him like a brother, and Alice and Gabriel cared for him. His adoptive parents and siblings did, too, even though they had their own lives and never pushed to see him. They knew him. They'd known him as a sixteen-year-old kicked out by his parents. They realized how painful that wound still was, and they did their best not to dig it deeper. Asher had no such claims, but maybe it was for the best.

Maddox would never reach out to anyone if he had a choice, or at least he wouldn't have. He knew it was wrong now. He realized it hurt people. It probably hurt Asher, too, but he pushed through it to get to Maddox. And Maddox had always pushed back. It had been safer for him. It had stopped him from really living, though. He loved his job and his animals, but was that really enough? Most days, he'd say yes.

But now there was Brandon to consider, and Maddox couldn't stop thinking about what their life together might be like. If they bonded, if Brandon never left, they could be happy. Was Maddox selfish for not trying at the very least?

Hell, yes, he was.

Brandon stroked along one of Maddox's ears, and Maddox had to stop himself from leaning into the touch.

"I wish you'd let me in. I don't expect you to fall in love with me and want to bond right away. *I* don't want to bond right now. There's the mess with Bart Miller, and I'm only eighteen. I barely know you. But I wish you'd let me get to know you. I know we'd be good together. We wouldn't be mates otherwise. The bond isn't going to mean anything if you don't let me in, though." Brandon sighed. "I'm not going to stop trying, but I wish you'd make things easier on me. I don't have any experience in this, and I don't want to mess things up and send you running."

He wouldn't, but Maddox couldn't tell him that. He couldn't say anything right now without revealing he was awake. Maybe that would be the best thing to do, but Maddox's head was spinning with Brandon's words and the realization that Maddox was lonely and that it was his own damn fault.

Brandon gave Maddox's head one last scratch and left the bedroom. Maddox listened to his footsteps, holding his breath. Was Brandon going to leave? He shouldn't, not with Bart Miller still out there possibly hunting him, but maybe he didn't want to stick around anymore. He'd said he was going to keep trying to get through to Maddox, but would he really? Maddox didn't feel he was worth it, but Brandon clearly cared about their bond and the fact that they were mates.

Maddox shifted as soon as he heard the sound of the TV. He grabbed the clothes he'd left on the floor next to the bed, gave Prince Whiskerton's head an apologizing stroke, and picked up his phone from the nightstand and called Asher, praying he'd answer. It was the middle of the day, so he was at work, but they worked with animals who didn't care about them answering their phones.

"Maddox? Is everything okay?"

Asher sounded worried, and it surprised Maddox. "Of course."

"Oh, thank fuck. I thought something had happened since you never call."

"That's not true."

"Yeah, it is. So nothing's wrong?"

"No. I just . . . need advice."

"Oh. I see. Okay, what do you need from me? I'm ready for anything. I hope it's not sex advice because I don't want to imagine you and Brandon going at it, but I can deal with it if that's what you need."

Asher did care for Maddox, didn't he? Maddox had been so busy pushing him away that he'd never noticed. "It's not sex advice. We're not there yet. I need to know how to get close to him."

"I guess you don't mean in the physical sense?"

Maddox rolled his eyes. "No, I don't." Asher spent too much time with Terry. He was starting to sound like him.

"What made you decide you want him in your life?"

Maddox sighed. He'd expected to have to answer those kinds of questions before getting the advice he needed. "He's my mate. If I have to trust someone enough to believe they won't leave, he's the one. Especially if we bond."

"You shouldn't bond just because you want to be sure he won't leave."

"I never said we would do that. And again, we're not there yet."

"Right. Okay, so you want to spend time with him and get to know him, right? And you can't leave the house. How about pizza and a movie?"

"And where would I get pizza if I can't order it?"

"Don't fuck with me. I know your freezer is full of pizza."

It was. "That's it? Pizza and a movie?"

"Things don't have to be complicated, Maddox. This is what getting to know each other means. You spend time together, watch movies, listen to music, and sometimes, you talk about stuff like books or whatever. It's all small steps, and before you realize it, you're in love and want to spend the rest of your life with him."

Maddox wasn't sure he believed it really was that easy, but he supposed he was about to find out.

Brandon didn't look up when he heard Maddox come down the stairs. He didn't want to look eager or appear clingy, and as far as he knew, Maddox was just going to the kitchen to get something to eat. It was almost lunchtime, so it made sense. He'd also probably ask Brandon if he wanted anything just because he was a nice guy, no matter how strained things were between them.

Sure enough, Maddox appeared at the living room door. Brandon made sure not to look at him and stared at the TV even though he had no clue what he was watching.

"I'm putting pizza in the oven for lunch. Do you want some?" Maddox asked.

Brandon let himself look at Maddox. "Yes, thank you."

Maddox smiled. He didn't do it often, which was a pity, and Brandon cherished it. "Why are the people on TV naked?"

Brandon blinked. "What?"

"They're naked. The man and the woman. And in what looks like a forest. What are you watching, Brandon?"

Brandon had no idea what Maddox was talking about. He looked at the TV, his eyes widening when he saw a naked woman talking to a just as naked man. The important bits were hidden by unfocused spots and the bags they were both carrying. "It's a show."

Maddox smiled again. "I can see that. I was just wondering what kind of show it is."

"I . . . it's about people in the forest." Brandon had no idea why they were naked, though.

Maddox hesitated. Was he going to ask Brandon to change the channel? Brandon wouldn't care. He had no idea what was going on, and he could do without seeing those people's asses.

"I was thinking about watching a movie," Maddox finally said.

"Oh. Do you want me to leave? I can go to my bedroom."

"No, no. Stay."

Brandon frowned. "Who's coming?"

"Coming?"

"To watch the movie." Most people were at work. Lee and Nathalie should have been at school, but they'd been allowed to take a week off to get over what had happened. Brandon might have been the one who'd been assaulted, but they'd been in the club, too, and Lee had seen Brandon drugged up. Brandon knew he had nightmares, and he hated it

"I don't—"

"Because I'd like to invite my friends, too. Lee and Nathalie. They were here earlier, but they wouldn't mind coming back." They'd be delighted, especially Lee, and Brandon wasn't sure he wanted to spend time on his own with Maddox and his friends. He'd never seen him with them before, but he could easily imagine he'd be an outsider. He didn't want to watch Maddox be happy and lively with his friends and know he couldn't have that.

Maddox rubbed the back of his neck. "Sure. Call them and ask them to come. I'll throw more pizza in the oven."

He disappeared into the kitchen, and Brandon texted Lee and Nathalie. He knew one of them would see the text, and he wasn't surprised Lee answered. He lived with his phone in his hand. *I'll come, but Nat had to go.*

She hadn't mentioned anything, but it wasn't like they never did anything without one of them, so Brandon didn't think twice about it. He changed the channel on the TV and thought about what kind of movie Maddox might want to watch. Anything with naked people was out, though. Brandon did *not* need that kind of awkwardness.

Lee was the first to arrive, followed by one of Maddox's friends, Gabriel. Gabriel disappeared into the kitchen, and Brandon forced himself to keep his ass on the couch. Lee leaned closer. "He's cute. Do you know who he is?"

"Just his name."

"But he's your mate's friend. That means we're going to spend time together."

Brandon rolled his eyes. "I guess. He's ten years older than you, though."

"And Maddox is ten years older than you. So what?"

"Nothing." Brandon knew age was just a number, and that it wouldn't change the fact that he and Maddox were mates, but he wasn't used to hanging out with people that much older than him—his parents didn't count. His friends were all around his age, and while he knew some of the older people in the pack, he wasn't friends with them.

The last one to arrive was Alice. Brandon didn't ask about Asher even though he knew he was Maddox's best friend. He was no doubt at work, so his absence made sense. Brandon was surprised Alice and Gabriel had managed to come, but he didn't ask how.

They picked a crime movie and settled to watch, but no one seemed very interested in what was happening on the screen. Alice kept sneaking glances at Brandon and grinning at him when their gazes met. Gabriel was more discreet, but he looked at Brandon often. He spent a lot of time leaning close to Maddox and softly talking to him.

Lee was the one who broke the ice. "This movie is shit."

Alice's smile widened. "Is it?"

"Yeah. It's obvious who the killer is."

"Is it?"

That would keep the conversation going—Brandon knew Lee loved anything with murder and blood, and he'd probably watched every movie available. It had been hard to find one he hadn't seen yet, but Brandon wasn't surprised Lee didn't like it. He was hard to please when it came to crime movies and TV series.

"What do you think of it?" Gabriel asked Brandon.

Brandon wasn't sure why he was talking to him, but he needed to make an effort. If there was any kind of future for him and Maddox, his three friends would be in Brandon's life. They were there to stay, and he wanted them to like him. "I'm not sure. I trust Lee when he says the movie isn't good, though. He knows what he's talking about."

"He's a movie buff?"

"A crime movie buff."

"What about you?"

Brandon shrugged. "I can take it or leave it. I'd rather watch superhero movies, but I don't mind."

"Superheroes, huh? Which one is your favorite?"

"Captain America, of course."

Gabriel's smile widened, and he elbowed Maddox in the side. "Hear that? Same as you. You two can bond over your shared love of Captain America."

Maddox's cheeks flushed. Brandon hoped it wasn't because he was trying to find a way to say no without offending him.

Maddox cleared his throat. "I'll get the DVDs out. We can watch it together."

Brandon would have thought he was talking with Gabriel if he hadn't been looking right at him. He gave Maddox a tentative smile and nodded. "That would be great. I kind of have a lot of time to kill right now."

"So do I."

Things were more relaxed after that quick conversation. Lee grumbled his way through the rest of the movie, and of course, he'd been right about the killer. Maddox turned the TV off, and they all sat back. Brandon had eaten too much pizza, but he didn't mind. He liked feeling drowsy and full, especially with Maddox looking at him the way he was. Brandon wasn't sure what way that was, but as long as Maddox looked at him, he was happy.

Maddox had relaxed during the movie, and he was still smiling.

"How about another movie?" Lee asked. "I'm picking it this time."

They all looked at each other. It would be dinner time soon, but Brandon wouldn't mind staying where he was. He liked Maddox's friends. They hadn't talked much, but they were treating him and Lee like they were part of their group.

Alice got up and stretched. "As long as I buy takeout for dinner."

"Takeout isn't safe for Brandon," Maddox pointed out. "But I'll call Asher and see if he and Terry want to come. He can stop on his way and buy something to eat. In the meantime, we can all use the bathroom, and I have to take the dogs out."

"Sounds like a plan."

They disbanded for a while. Lee followed Brandon to his bedroom but didn't tease or ask anything about Maddox and how the day was going. They both used the bathroom, and Brandon straightened his clothes. He wanted to look good for Maddox, although he doubted Maddox would care.

He felt like they'd taken a step forward, though. It was a small one, but he couldn't wait to see where it took them.

Maddox hoped no one noticed how often he was looking at Brandon. He'd tried focusing on the movie, but he hadn't even realized it was a crime movie until Lee had mentioned it. His mind was entirely on Brandon.

"It's going well, isn't it?" Gabriel asked.

They were in the kitchen getting drinks. Asher and Terry had just arrived and were taking the containers of food out of the bags. Everyone was gathering in the living room again. Maddox couldn't remember the last time that he'd had so many people in his home. Probably never, actually. Gabriel, Alice, Asher, and sometimes Terry came often, but everyone else gave Maddox space, including his adoptive family. He was glad for it, but now he realized that maybe having people around wasn't that bad.

He shrugged. "I think it is. No one's killing anyone."

Gabriel rolled his eyes. "Why would something like that happen?"

"We're putting together two groups of friends who never had contact before. I wouldn't have been surprised if there'd been some clashing."

Gabriel shook his head. "There won't be. Brandon and Lee are great, and our group will accept them. Brandon's your mate. He has a place with us."

Maddox was glad to hear that. He was more and more convinced that maybe he *could* have Brandon in his life. He certainly wanted to, although he still wasn't sure up to what point or what he was ready for. He knew he'd have to take things slow. No matter how much his caracal wanted to grab Brandon and sink their fangs into his neck, Maddox couldn't do that.

But he could open up a bit more. He could give Brandon a chance.

He and Gabriel went back to the living room. Some of the cats and all three dogs had drifted there, no doubt hoping for some of the food, so Maddox glared at the humans in the room. "No food to the animals," he warned, looking especially at Alice, who was already handing a piece of meat to Colonel Bau.

She bit her lower lip. "But he's looking at me with those

eyes."

"Those are his eyes, and he can't very well change them. Stop teaching my pets to beg for food. I feed them, so they're not hungry."

"I know that. You're a responsible furry dad."

Maddox blinked. "Let's not talk about being a furry dad again, please. It sounds weird." And sexual, but if no one brought it up, Maddox wasn't going to. Maybe he just had a weird mind.

Everyone started to settle down, fighting with the pets over the couches and armchairs. Maddox sat next to Queen Elizabeth, who gave him a haughty glance and started licking her paw. She wasn't going anywhere, so Maddox slid as close to her as he could without losing a finger to give space to whoever would sit next to him.

Brandon did.

Maddox looked up when Brandon came closer and flopped into the empty space. Of course, King McFluff decided to sit on Brandon's other side, which meant he and Maddox were pressed together, their thighs touching, their movements awkward. Their elbows kept bumping together as they ate, and Maddox had to fight the urge to apologize every time.

Lee put on another movie while Terry turned the main light off, leaving only the small one on the side table on. It wasn't completely dark, but the atmosphere had gone from energized with laughter and chats to cozy and intimate. It wasn't hard for Maddox to imagine him and Brandon there alone, watching TV and cuddling.

Maddox was aware of every movement Brandon made. He couldn't remember the last time he'd felt this way, and it was both uncomfortable and exciting.

He didn't pay any more attention to this movie than he had to the first one. He didn't even try, not with Brandon so close to him.

They seemed to gravitate even closer to each other as the time passed. Maddox hadn't thought it possible, not when they'd already been pressed together, but it felt like Brandon was everywhere.

"Sorry," he muttered.

Maddox frowned. "What for?"

"You know. Being so close. It's just that I don't want to move King McFluff."

Maddox could have told him to move the cat without worrying about it, but he didn't. Instead, he said, "It's fine. I don't mind."

It was the right thing to do, because Brandon's smile was sweet and happy. "No?"

"No. It's nice. Cozy. I like it."

Brandon leaned even closer. "The movie?"

They were whispering so they wouldn't disturb the others, but Maddox didn't miss the quick glance and thumbs up Asher gave him. His first reaction was to roll his eyes, but he didn't want Brandon to think it was at him, so he didn't. "I'm sure the movie is nice, but it's not what I was talking about."

Brandon licked his lips. "What were you talking about, then?"

Maddox didn't want to go into what he'd been thinking, not with so many other people around them. He also didn't want to completely back off, though. He needed to make Brandon understand he wasn't fighting them anymore, but without going into details because this wasn't the time and place.

Gosh, he felt so awkward. Even when he hooked up — and he did so only rarely — he never knew what to do. With Brandon, it was forever, so it always freaked Maddox out. What if he did something wrong and Brandon thought he was awkward or whatever? He wouldn't be wrong, but Maddox didn't want him to see.

Still, he needed to do something. He wriggled his arm from between them and held it up, silently looking at Brandon. Brandon's eyes were wide, but he nodded slightly and settled against Maddox's side. Maddox wrapped his arm around Brandon's shoulder and squeezed.

They both turned back to the TV, but it was even harder to focus now. Maddox had no idea what was going on in the movie or who the characters were. With Brandon so close to him, his scent wrapping around Maddox, there was no way Maddox could even think about anything that wasn't him.

And that was surprisingly okay with him. He'd been fighting this so hard, staying away from Brandon and finding excuses for them not to work, that he hadn't thought about how good things could be if he let them happen.

Brandon was young, there was no changing that, but it didn't mean it was a bad thing. They didn't have to rush into anything just because they were mates. They could take their time, get to know each other. Until Bart Miller was caught, Brandon wasn't going anywhere, so they had time. Maddox would have to go back to work sooner rather than later, but in the meantime, he was going to seek out Brandon rather than avoid him.

"Are you okay?" Brandon asked.

Maddox looked down at him. Who cared about the movie anyway? "I am. Why?"

"I don't know. You're behaving differently from what I'm used to tonight."

"I decided to stop fighting."

Brandon blinked. "Fighting? You mean us?"

"Yes."

"Why?"

Maddox shook his head. "Not now."

"All right."

Maddox's hand was trembling when he reached up to touch Brandon's cheek. Brandon's eyes widened, and his lips parted, but he stayed still. Maddox cupped his cheek. His heart was racing as if this were his first kiss, and he supposed that in a way, it was. It would be his last first kiss, and Brandon's.

Maybe this wasn't the best place or time, with their friends surrounding them, but a quick look around told Maddox that either they all found the film incredibly interesting, or they were doing their best to give him and Brandon privacy. Either way, it didn't matter. They weren't looking at them, and Maddox was going to take advantage of that.

Because he felt warm and cozy, surrounded by friends and their love. He'd always tried so hard to push them away, and he wasn't going to stop spending a lot of his time on his own, but he knew they weren't ever going to leave or reject him. They were there to stay, and so was Brandon.

Maddox leaned down and brushed their lips together. Brandon stayed still as if afraid Maddox would spook if he moved, so Maddox rubbed his fingertips on Brandon's neck, coaxing him closer. He kissed Brandon again, and this time Brandon kissed him back.

It was soft and gentle, and perfect. Maddox wasn't going to deepen the kiss, not here and now, but he didn't need to. It already gave him everything he wanted.

CHAPTER SIX

Brandon couldn't stop smiling. He hadn't been able to stop since movie night two days ago, and he doubted he would anytime soon. He didn't *want* to, either.

His life was going well, except for that being hunted thing. Honestly, he didn't think Bart Miller was still after him. If it had been him, he'd have left town as soon as he'd escaped, and why wouldn't Bart? It was what made the most sense. Why would he want to get to Brandon when he was free and could stay free as long as he left town?

But Brandon wasn't the one who made decisions in this case. Both Kameron and Patrick wanted him to stay where he was, and it wasn't a hardship, not when it meant spending his days with Maddox. Of course, he wished he could also go out with him, even if it was only to go grocery shopping. That was where Maddox was right now, and Brandon wasn't sure what to do with himself.

He was spread out on the couch with Queen Elizabeth snuggled against his side and Lord Nibbles on his chest purring like crazy. It felt like every time Brandon sat down, one or more cats decided to use him as a pillow. He didn't mind it, though. He hadn't had pets growing up, and he liked feeling like he was never alone. Of course, he could have done without that when he was in the bathroom, but he supposed that came with the territory.

Brandon didn't want to wake up Lord Nibbles, but he'd had enough of lazing on the couch. Maddox had left about half an hour ago, so he was bound to come back soon. Maybe Brandon could start lunch so they'd only have to sit down once they were both home? He wasn't a great cook, but he could handle some pasta with a simple sauce, and he thought Maddox would be glad to find food ready once he got back.

Brandon gently put Lord Nibbles next to Queen Elizabeth. He held his breath and prayed they wouldn't try to tear each other's head off, but they settled down after meowing a few times.

He headed to the kitchen and put on some water to boil, but a knock on the door interrupted him. He paused, wondering who it was. It could be one of their friends. They were used to coming around. Although, Maddox had admitted they didn't do it often because he'd always been so prickly. It *was* weird that they'd come at this hour of the day, especially since Maddox had confessed that he'd invited Alice and Gabriel over the other day only because Brandon hadn't realized he wanted to watch a movie with him *alone*.

Maybe Brandon shouldn't open the door. If it was one of their friends, they'd understand. It could be important, though. Maybe it was Kameron or Patrick coming to tell him Bart Miller had been caught? Or maybe it was Brandon's mom or dad who wanted to check in on him. He was surprised his mom hadn't come around yet. If it was her, she was going to freak out if he didn't open. She'd probably call the police, SWAT, and everyone else she could reach, and that was the last thing Brandon needed. He had to hide, not put a spotlight on the house where he was staying.

There was another knock, and Brandon could already see his mom pound harder and yell at him to open. He rushed to the door and swung it open, his lips already moving to tell her off, but it was Nathalie.

Brandon blinked at her. "Hey. What are you doing here?"

She licked her lips and looked around. "Is Maddox

home?"

"No. What's wrong?" She looked even worse than she had the last time they'd seen each other.

In the beginning, Brandon had put it up to what had happened to him, but he doubted that was it. Her eyes were red, and she was biting her lip so hard Brandon half expected her to bite it off. She was hugging herself as if she were cold, but the weather wasn't that bad, so that couldn't be it. She was too pale, and Brandon stepped aside. "What happened, Nat?" he asked.

She stayed on the porch. "I'm sorry."

"What for?"

She licked her lips again. "I didn't want to do it, but he said he'd give me enough to get through the week if I did. He promised he won't hurt you. He just wanted to talk to you."

"You're not making sense, Nat. Who are you talking about? Who's not going to hurt me?" Because usually when someone promised not to hurt you, you could be damn sure they would. Brandon didn't like what was happening, but he wasn't even sure what it was.

Nathalie looked behind her. Brandon swallowed and followed her gaze. A man was climbing the porch steps, and he knew who it was before he even saw him. He didn't remember much of what had happened that night at the club, not after he'd been drugged, but he'd seen Bart Miller at the police station. He'd hoped he'd never have to see him again, yet there he was.

Brandon tried to slam the door shut, but Nathalie pushed herself into the house. "I'm sorry, Bran, I'm sorry."

Brandon didn't know why she was doing this — it didn't make sense — but he wasn't going to stop to find out. He could ask questions later, once he was safe and Bart had been dealt with.

He tried to push the door shut again, but Nathalie wasn't budging, so he let go and ran toward the back of the house, praying the dogs weren't going to come see what was happening. There was no way to tell what Miller would do to them if they did, and Brandon didn't want to risk it.

He'd left his phone on the table in the kitchen, so he ran that way. He could snatch the phone and exit through the back door. Hopefully, he'd manage to get into the woods before Miller got to him.

Something grabbed his shirt and pulled him back. A flash of dark hair told him it was Bart Miller and that he wasn't going to make it to his phone. His heart sank, but he struggled anyway. He wasn't going to go down easily. Miller might have managed to knock him out once, but that was because he'd been drugged. He wasn't now, and while he wasn't sure what he could do, he was going to try anything.

And since Bart Miller had drugged him to rape him, Brandon shifted. He hoped the man wasn't into sex with animals, and this way, he could use his fangs.

Miller had to let go when Brandon shifted, but he didn't leave. Brandon turned toward him, barring his fangs, but the only thing that got him was laughter. Bart was *amused*.

"You're cute, little wolf. Cuter in your human form, though, so it's a pity I won't be able to fuck you like I was planning to."

Brandon wanted to curl up and hide from the malice and hatred in Miller's voice, but he didn't move. He wouldn't have many chances to do this. Maybe he could manage to run outside and hide in the forest, or even in another room and lock himself in. He'd have to shift back to do that, but it might be worth the risk.

Miller reached for him, and Brandon stepped back. He snarled, hearing an answering snarl behind Miller. Colonel Bau was there, and Brandon's heart hurt. Was Miller going to hurt the sweet dog?

Miller didn't even seem to notice. He reached for Brandon again, and this time, Brandon was too slow, focused as he was on Colonel Bau. Miller grabbed Brandon's fur and pulled him closer.

Brandon snapped his mouth shut, catching Miller's arm. Miller swore and let go, but before Brandon could turn and run, something hit him on the head from behind. The pain made him gasp, and he fell. He scrambled to get back to his feet, but Miller pushed him down and kicked him.

"That's for biting me, bitch. And now you'll pay, just like I said you would."

Brandon curled in on himself as Miller kicked him again and again. He heard barking and growls, and even now, he hoped the dogs would be okay. If something had to happen to him, if he didn't make it, at least Maddox would have them.

Maddox grabbed two of the bags from the trunk and trudged toward the house, praying they wouldn't break. It always happened when he had fragile things like eggs in them.

He climbed the porch steps and smiled when he saw the open door. "Hey, I didn't think you'd hear me," he said, pushing the door open wider with his ass as he stepped in. He'd expected to find Brandon there waiting for him, or coming toward him to help, but the entrance was empty.

Had Brandon forgotten to close the door? But that didn't make sense. He hadn't left the house since he'd moved in, and he'd promised he wouldn't until Bart Miller was caught. And if he had, wouldn't he have made sure the door was closed?

"Brandon?" Maddox called out. He closed the door with

his foot. Where were the dogs? They always came to the door when he came back home. Most of the time, the cats were right there with him, yet now, none of them were in sight.

Maddox's heart raced as he walked to the kitchen. He wasn't sure what he'd expected to see, but it wasn't an empty room. There was a steaming pot on the stove, and he turned the heat under if off once he'd put the bags down.

"Brandon?" he called out again.

There was a meow, and King McFluff came in. He didn't come to Maddox like he usually did, staying by the door instead. When Maddox reached for him, he ran away.

That wasn't normal behavior. Something had spooked him.

Maddox swallowed and went through every room of the house. He found all four cats hidden under beds and Colonel Bau and Madam Mimsy behind the couch. Princess Pawpington was cowering in her crate, but she came out when she saw him, licking his face as he ran his hands over her to make sure she was okay. The fact that all of them had stayed inside was a small miracle, but the fact that Brandon was nowhere to be seen meant Maddox wasn't as relieved as he might have been in other circumstances.

"Brandon?" he called one last time even though he now knew for sure that Brandon wasn't in the house.

Maddox took his phone out and called Asher. He should have called Patrick or Kameron, but his brain was stuck on the fact that Brandon wasn't home. He couldn't think past the fear.

"Hey, Maddox. What's up? Are we watching another movie tonight?" Asher answered.

"Brandon isn't home."

"Oh? Maybe he went to visit his parents, or to see his friends?"

"The door was open when I came back. The cats and the dogs were all inside, but they could have snuck out. He wouldn't leave the door open. Besides, there was a pot on the stove. No, something happened to him." Maddox could feel it, even though they weren't bonded.

"Okay. Hang up and call Kam. I'll call Patrick."

The conversation with Kameron went pretty much like the one with Asher had gone, and once he'd hung up, Maddox found himself at a loss. Kameron had told him to stay where he was, so he sat on the couch. The dogs crowded around him, and he petted them, trying to breathe and release the tension.

It rocketed right up when there was a brisk knock on the door and Kameron walked in before Maddox could answer.

"I've already put the guard on alert and asked Bran to dispatch at least one team of enforcers," he said. They'll be here in seconds."

Maddox wasn't even upset when a group of people shimmered into his living room. They could have shimmered into the bathroom while he was showering, and he wouldn't have cared, either, not right now.

"Bran told you?" Kameron asked.

One of the men nodded. "Yes. I'm going to shift and sniff around if that's okay with everyone."

He'd already started taking his clothes off, and no one protested. Maddox made a strangled sound when the man shifted into a werewolf rather than an animal, but he didn't care. The guy could have been a purple cow, and as long as he could find Brandon, Maddox would have been fine with it.

"Jackson will find your mate," Kameron said, but it wasn't reassuring.

Maddox wished it was. He didn't want his brain to bring up the worst scenarios like it had been doing since he'd come home.

Another man approached Maddox, crouching in front of him. From his long blond hair and his green eyes, Maddox knew he was a Nix, the Nix who'd shimmered the others inside. "Hi. I'm Mael. I'd like to try to find your mate through you. It's the fastest way to get to him."

Maddox licked his lips. "What do you need me to do?"

"I'm going to take your hand. I need you to close your eyes and think about your mate. Focus on him."

It was hard, harder than Maddox expected. He kept thinking about what was happening to Brandon right now, and he had to force his mind away from that. Mael didn't say anything, though. He gave him time, even when the werewolf came back in and told Kameron that the trail stopped in front of the house, probably where a car had been waiting.

The only way to find Brandon was through Mael—through Maddox. Maddox had to stop freaking out.

He took a deep breath and thought about Brandon's face. His cheeks were always flushed after they made out, and it was endearing. They seemed to be kissing all the time now that they'd started, and Maddox loved it. He hated having waited so long, but if he got Brandon back, he'd make sure Brandon knew he wanted him forever. They wouldn't bond, not yet, because making sure Brandon didn't disappear again wasn't a good enough reason to do it, but Maddox was going to ask Brandon to move in with him permanently. They fit well together, and Brandon belonged in Maddox's house.

"I have him," Mael said.

Maddox opened his eyes.

Mael smiled at him and let go of his hands, rising to his feet.

"Where is he?" Maddox asked.

"Not far from here, in town. He's moving, so he's probably still in the car Jackson talked about."

Kameron nodded. "Go."

"I want to go with you," Maddox blurted out.

He knew there was pity in Mael's gaze when he looked at him, and he was glad Mael didn't try to make him feel better. He knew he was stupid even to think he could go with them, but he hated the thought off staying home and wait to find out what had happened to his mate.

"I'm sorry, Maddox," Kameron said gently. "I know why you want to go, and trust me, I wish I could say yes, but you're not an enforcer. They know what they're doing. They'll neutralize the danger and bring Brandon home. I promise."

"How can you be sure? How do you know he's okay?"

"I don't, but if he' still moving, I doubt that whoever has him wasted time hurting him. They have a place, and the sooner we get Brandon back, the better it will be." Kameron looked at the enforcers. "Go. We'll stay here, so let us know if you're taking Brandon to the infirmary once you have him."

Maddox didn't even want to think about why they would take him there. He couldn't, not unless he wanted to freak out again, and in front of Kameron this time.

The enforcers disappeared just as the front door slammed open. Asher ran in, frantic, relaxing when he saw Maddox. He rushed toward him and pulled him into his arms, and for once, Maddox didn't protest. He needed the contact and affection Asher was giving him. He couldn't keep his best friend at arm's length this time, not when he might just have lost half his life, a half he hadn't known he needed before he'd found it.

"He'll be okay," Asher said.

Maddox wanted to believe him. He nodded, unable to get

a word out, and swallowed. He had to do something to pass the time. Hopefully Brandon would be home soon, but in the meantime, Maddox had things to do. "I need to check the animals," he croaked.

Asher moved away and nodded. "I'll help you. What do you need me to do?"

"Check they're unharmed. I didn't have time to do that yet." It wasn't much, but it would take Maddox's mind off Brandon and what was happening to him right now.

Brandon's head hurt. He was pretty sure Nathalie had hit him with something, and he was going to kick her ass as soon as he could.

Okay, so maybe he'd just yell at her, for that and for bringing Bart Miller with her. What the fuck had she been thinking? Brandon was angry, and his first instinct was to never talk to her again, but he wanted to know what was going on.

Of course, he wasn't going to find out until he freed himself

He was pretty sure he was in the back of Miller's car. He was in his human form again—he'd shifted after Miller had kicked him repeatedly—and wrapped him in a blanket with his face covered. He wasn't sure why Miller had bothered, but he was grateful. This would be much worse if he was bare ass naked. He wanted to shift again, but the pounding in his head made it difficult to focus. His wolf was in as much pain as he was, and while it was pushing forward, neither of them were doing a great job of it.

He tried to touch his head, but he was tied up under the blanket, and no matter how hard he struggled, there was no budging the ropes. He felt like a burrito about to be eaten. The fact that he couldn't do anything was terrifying.

The car stopped. Brandon screwed his eyes shut, but it was like a child not looking at something he was afraid of. It didn't change the fact that he'd been hit and kidnapped, and that if Miller had his way, he'd be dead by the end of the day.

"Can I have it now?"

Brandon blinked. He hadn't realized Nathalie was in the car with them.

"Stop asking," Miller snapped.

Brandon gritted his teeth. The man even sounded like an asshole. How had Nathalie met him? And why did she associate with him?

"Stay in the car. I need to buy some stuff. I'll give you everything I have on me once I'm back. Don't let him out, because if you do, I'll kill you in his place," Miller said.

One of the car doors opened, the car rocked, and the door closed. Brandon held his breath, hoping that meant Miller was gone. He didn't know why or where they were, but he hoped he could get through to Nathalie.

He opened one of his eyes and winced. Even with his face covered, the light that filtered through hurt his eyes. That hit on the head had been bad. He'd even lost consciousness for a bit, and he'd been groggy since then, enough that he hadn't been able to fight back when he'd been carried out of Maddox's house.

God, Maddox. He was going to freak out when he came home and found Brandon gone. He was so scared of Brandon leaving him. Brandon hoped he'd realize he hadn't gone willingly, but he had no way to know how Bart and Nathalie had left the house. If they were smart, and Nathalie was, usually, they'd have cleaned up so it looked like Brandon had left.

Brandon cleared his throat. "Nat?" he croaked.

He heard her suck in a breath. Then she asked, "You're

awake?"

Brandon rolled his eyes. "Yeah. What's going on, Nat? Where are we? Why did you bring Bart Miller to my house? How do you even know him? And could you please take off whatever's on my face? I can't breathe." That wasn't true, but he wanted to see, and he guessed that was the easiest way to obtain that.

"He's going to get angry."

"You can cover me up again when he comes back. Please." Brandon needed to see where they were. He wasn't sure he'd be able to from his position stretched on the back seat, but maybe he could see the top of the buildings or whatever. He'd take any hint.

He heard Nathalie move and held his breath. The cloth on his face slid away, and he blinked his eyes open. He could see the ceiling of the car and Nathalie's face, but she disappeared almost right away, sliding back in her seat.

Brandon swallowed. "Why are you doing this, Nat? Did he threaten you? Did he hurt you?" That was Brandon's worst fear.

She shook her head. She wouldn't look at Brandon, so he knew it was bad. He'd already known, of course. The fact that he was trussed up like a pig in the backseat of a car had pointed that way since the beginning.

"What is it, then?" he pushed. He was still hoping to get through to her and to convince her to let him go, and he doubted he'd have much time to do it. He couldn't convince her of anything if he didn't know what was going on, though.

Nathalie bounced her knee. "I need him."

"For what? Please, tell me he's not your boyfriend."

She snorted. "Of course not." She took a deep breath and turned her head to look at Brandon. "He's my dealer."

Brandon blinked. "Your dealer?"

"Yes. I'm . . . I take drugs, sometimes." She shrugged. "It's fun."

"It's *fun*? So fun that you're selling one of your best friends to an asshole so he can rape and probably kill me? *Fun?*"

Her cheeks flushed. "He promised not to hurt you. He's just going to scare you or something."

"And you believe that?" When had this happened? How could he not have noticed? Nathalie, Lee, and he were best friends. It was true they weren't as close as they used to be as kids, but they were still best friends, or at least Brandon had thought so.

Nathalie tugged on a strand of hair. "I have to believe it. I need him."

"Why didn't you talk to Lee or to me Nat? You could have told us about this drug problem, and we would have helped you. You know that."

"I don't have a drug problem. It's just for fun."

She was fooling herself, and she probably knew it. Brandon wasn't going to push, though. He needed her to let him go, and she wasn't going to do that if she was angry. "Okay, not a problem. Sorry. There has to be another way to get your fix, though. What about other dealers? There's no way Bart is the only one in town." Not with the ODs that had been happening lately.

"Of course there are other dealers, but he has an in with the Beasts. They have the best stuff."

Brandon's stomach dropped. Everyone knew the Beasts, but they'd never been seen in Gillham. Had they arrived here? Brandon didn't know, and right now, he didn't care. If Miller was a Beast, things weren't going to go well for Brandon.

He had to get out of the car. "Nathalie, let me out. He's going to hurt me if you don't."

"He's not. He promised."

"Don't be an idiot. He promised because he needed you to show him where I was. You wouldn't have if he'd told you he was planning to kill me." Or at least Brandon hoped she wouldn't have. She was clinging to that promise because she knew it was bullshit and she had to believe it to make this right.

"He's coming back."

Brandon swore. "Nat, please."

She turned around, and Brandon thought she was going to untie him. Instead, she smiled sadly at him and covered his face again. "He's going to hurt me, too, if I don't help him."

"Nat, for fuck's sake!"

The car door opened, and Brandon snapped his mouth shut. He needed to do something, anything to get out of this situation.

"Don't talk to him," Miller growled.

"He was just saying he couldn't breathe."

"He's not going to breathe for much longer anyway."

"But you said —"

"Shut up, bitch." The car dipped under Miller's weight. "What the fuck?" he yelped.

There was a dragging sound, and Miller yelled again. Nathalie wasn't saying anything, and Brandon needed that fucking cloth off his face. He had to know what was happening. "Nat? What's going on?"

She didn't answer. He heard the door on her side of the car open, and he knew she'd left. He swallowed. Had Miller told her to leave so he could kill him? The car hadn't moved, so he'd have to drive to somewhere more private. Brandon's chances to make it were slim without her help, though.

The back door next to his head open, and he held his breath, praying it wasn't Miller. The cloth was pulled away, and a man with long blond hair and pointed ears looked down at him. "Brandon?" he asked.

He was wearing the enforcers' uniform, and Brandon would have hugged him if he hadn't been tied up. "Yes."

The man smiled. "I'm Mael. I'm here to take you home to your mate."

Maddox was on his feet as soon as Mael shimmered into his living room, holding hands with Brandon. Brandon was wrapped in a blanket, and one of his eyes was swollen, but he looked otherwise okay. Maddox rushed to him, slowing down only when he gathered him into his arms. "Are you okay?"

Brandon blinked up at Maddox. "Mostly, yeah."

"You need a doctor."

"I can heal his eye," Mael said.

"Shouldn't you go back?"

Mael shrugged. "The others have the situation under control. The two aren't going anywhere."

Maddox frowned. "Two?" Bart Miller had been alone in that bathroom with Brandon, thank God, but of course, that didn't mean he didn't have contacts in town. Not everyone would be smart enough to say no if he asked for help.

"Yeah. The other one's a girl."

"It's Nathalie," Brandon whispered. He pressed his face against Maddox's chest and shuddered.

Maddox held him close and rubbed his back. "You mean, *your* Nathalie?"

"Yeah. Can we talk about it later? I don't want to right now."

"Of course." Maddox noticed Brandon's feet were bare. "You're naked." He'd known that, of course he had. He'd found Brandon's torn clothes in the kitchen, kicked under the table. Brandon had shifted to try to get away, but it hadn't worked.

"Yeah, sorry."

"Don't apologize. I was trying to ask if Miller — if he touched you." Maddox had to push the words out. He didn't want to say them. He didn't even want to think about them.

"No, no. He didn't. He did say he wanted to, you know, but he didn't have the time, especially not with Nathalie there."

Maddox wanted to find out what Nathalie had done, and possibly wring her neck for hurting Brandon. And it wasn't only that. Brandon was the most important part in this, of course, but Maddox had welcomed Nathalie in his home, and she'd used that to get to Brandon. She'd led a rapist drug dealer into his home knowing full well he'd hurt his mate. *This* was one of the reasons Maddox didn't like people. They couldn't be trusted, not even when you thought you knew them.

But he trusted Brandon, and he wanted him in his life. That wasn't going to change. It had taken him being kidnapped for Maddox to realize it. He didn't like it, but at least now he knew.

He was falling in love with Brandon. It was terrifying, but the possibility of losing him was even scarier. He'd resisted as hard as he could, but he'd fallen.

And he was happy about it.

Mael gestured at Brandon to come closer. Maddox didn't let his mate go, taking his hand and linking their fingers together. Brandon smiled at him and closed his eyes, and Mael raised his hand. The healing part didn't take long, but Maddox was still worried. "Can you tell if he has something else? There was a scuffle, right?"

"I'm fine," Brandon protested.

"How did they get you out of the house?" Even with two,

Brandon would probably have been able to kick and bite and maybe free himself, but at the very least, done some damage to the furniture and the various stuff around.

Brandon avoided Maddox's gaze. "Nathalie hit me with something. I might have lost consciousness for a bit, but it wasn't more than a few minutes."

Mael chuckled. "All right. Let me check your head. I can probably patch you up. It doesn't look bad. There's no blood or anything." He reached around Brandon and touched the back of his head. Brandon winced, but he didn't say anything. Mael's hand glowed, and the tension disappeared from Brandon's face.

"Better?" Mael asked as he dropped his hand.

Brandon opened his eyes. "Yes. Thank you."

Mael nodded. "All right. You can go to the infirmary if you need anything, of course. I'm going back."

"I'm coming with you," Kameron said.

Maddox had completely forgotten there were other people in the living room because he'd been so focused on Brandon. But of course Kameron and Asher were still there, and so Brandon's family and Lee. At least now they knew why they hadn't been able to find Nathalie.

Lee rushed to Brandon's side as soon as Kameron was gone. "What did she do to you?" he asked, looking like he might murder someone.

If that someone was Nathalie, Maddox was on board with that. He let go of Brandon's hand and stepped away to let Brandon's parents and Lee have access to him. He wasn't sure what to do with himself, and he was glad when Asher took his wrist and pulled him to the side.

"Once the reunion is over, you're going to take Brandon upstairs," Asher said. He was taking charge, and Maddox was glad for it. He was at a loss when it came to feelings and talking about them to people.

He nodded. "Okay." Brandon was bound to want some time on his own, right?

"He's going to want a shower and clean clothes. Take care of him. I'll get everyone out and make sure you have something to eat once you're done."

"But—"

Asher pressed a hand against Maddox's mouth. "Nope. No buts. I know this is your home and that you should be the one in charge, but you're not up to it. Let me take control. I promise you won't regret it. *Trust* me, Maddox. You can."

And Maddox did. He'd fought it for so long, but now he knew he could trust people—Brandon, Asher, Gabriel, Alice. The fear that they'd do something like what Nathalie had done was there, and he doubted it would go away for a while, but this was what trust was. He needed to let go and just . . . trust.

It took him a while to extricate Brandon from the small crowd around him, and he managed to do so only by pointing out that Brandon was still naked under the blanket he was clutching. Maddox was more than happy to leave everyone to Asher after that, especially Brandon's mother, who was still protesting the fact that Brandon was going upstairs rather than into her car to go home. Maddox didn't know how things would end up with Brandon, if he'd stay or if he'd leave now that Miller had been caught, but he wasn't going to bring it up now. No, the only thing he was going to do would be taking care of Brandon.

"Don't go?" Brandon asked before going into the bathroom.

"I'll wait for you here." Maddox knew Brandon had to be scared, worried, and horrified. He wasn't sure how to deal with all that, but he'd be there for his mate.

He was sitting on the bed when Brandon came out of the

bathroom. He was only wearing a towel, since they'd both forgotten to get him clothes, and Maddox looked away. He *wanted* to look, but now wasn't the right moment.

"Do you feel better?" he asked.

"Kinda. I was wondering if we could shift and snuggle? I kind of want a nap, and, well, I'd be more comfortable as a wolf."

"Of course." Maddox paused. "I'll just go to my room to undress and shift."

Brandon nodded. "Before you go, though."

"Yes?"

"I just . . . thank you for not thinking I'd left. You called the enforcers."

"I called Kameron, but yeah. And I can't deny the thought did pass through my mind."

"Yet you overcame it."

"I had to. I couldn't believe you'd go."

"I wouldn't. I want to stay here, Maddox. I know I should probably go home since I'm not in danger anymore, but I was already planning to move out of my mom's house. I *can* go to my dad's, but I've gotten used to living with you. I don't expect anything from you."

"Yes." Maddox could tell Brandon would continue to ramble if he didn't stop him. He did that when he was nervous.

Brandon blinked. "Yes?"

"You can stay here. You can have this room still, or you can move into mine if you think you're ready for that." He licked his lips. "I know we haven't done much more than kissing, and just like you, I don't expect anything from you, but I don't think I could stand being away from you right now, not after what happened. I'm not ready to bond, and I don't think we should yet, but I want you in my life. Forever." Brandon wouldn't leave until he had a good reason, and

Maddox would do whatever he had not to give him one.

Chapter Seven

"Are you sure you want to do this?"

Brandon didn't answer because he wasn't. He never wanted to see Bart Miller again, and if he had to, he wanted to see him behind bars and possibly on fire, screaming as he went back to Hell.

But instead of that, he was watching him through a one-way mirror in the Gillham police station. It could have been worse — he was pretty sure Bart knew he was there, watching, so the fact that he hadn't said anything directly to him was surprising — but not by much. This was Brandon's version of hell, and he wanted to go back home.

Home, with Maddox. Brandon was still staying with him, no matter how many times his mom had already tried to convince him to go back home. He knew he'd have to talk to her sooner rather than later, but there wasn't much he had to say to her. He wasn't going to change his mind. He'd been living with Maddox for a few weeks, and he hoped he'd be there for decades yet. His mom knew that, just like his dad did, but they were reacting to it in different ways. Brandon wasn't surprised. His dad knew what meeting your mate meant and what it was like, so he was bound to understand better.

Besides, it wasn't like living with Maddox had changed Brandon's life that much, not now that the rest of his life was back to normal. He was going to school again, and he'd be graduating at the end of the year. He shared Maddox's room now, and they'd finally had sex, but that was the only thing that had changed apart from Brandon's address and the fact that he'd lost one of his best friends. He still saw Lee every day, both in and out of school, but Nathalie had been arrested. Brandon didn't know if she'd have to stay in jail or if she'd be sent away so she could deal with her drug problem, and he didn't waste much time thinking about it. He still cared for her, but she'd hurt him worse than anyone else had ever done. Even what Bart had done to him wasn't comparable, because they hadn't been best friends.

"We can go home," Maddox murmured. He was like a wall beside Brandon, strong and there to support him if he needed it. He probably would eventually, depending on what he was about to hear.

He shook his head. "I need to do this. I need to know he's not going to get out again." There was no way Patrick would let him escape again, and with everything else the police had found while Bart had been on the run, Bart would directly from the interrogation room to the council jail. The only reason he wasn't already there even though he'd been arrested four days earlier was that Brandon had wanted to listen to this. He was lucky he knew Kameron and Patrick, because it wouldn't have been possible otherwise.

The door in the interrogation room opened. Brandon straightened and looked at Patrick as he walked in, a bunch of files in his hand. He put them onto the table and sat in front of Bart. Bart was handcuffed to the table, but he looked as smug as he had every time Brandon had seen him.

Patrick put a hand onto the files. "We know you're a dealer for the Beasts."

Bart snorted. "And you actually had to investigate to find that out? I could have told you."

Patrick ignored Bart's smartass answer. "We can see about a reduced sentence if you give us names and locations. Not for what you did to Brandon Miller, but for the dealing."

"No."

Brandon wasn't surprised, and he didn't think Patrick was, either. The Beasts weren't just a gang. They were ruthless and cruel, and they wouldn't think anything of killing Bart for talking. They wanted to take over the humans and the shifters who didn't agree with them. Brandon supposed that went for every gang, but the Beasts were shifters and Nix, so they might be able to infiltrate the jail and get to Bart. The council and the enforcers did their best to keep the place secure, but nothing was ever one hundred percent sure when it came to people who could pop in and out of a place or shift into tiny animals like mice.

Patrick leaned back in his chair. "You're that afraid of the Beasts?"

"You should be. They don't play around, you know. They're in Gillham for a reason, and they're not going to stop until they have what they want."

"And what is that?"

"They want to destroy the pack. Why do you think the drugs I've been dealing are killing so many people?"

"You just admitted to knowingly selling dangerous drugs to people."

"I might as well. I'm either never going to see the outside of the jail again or die soon, so what do I have to lose?"

"Give me a name, and I'll see if I can make your stay there comfortable."

Brandon expected Miller to refuse like he had earlier, so he was surprised when he frowned instead and asked, "Can you promise me I'll be protected?"

"As well as we can. The council jail isn't easily accessible, and if we put you in solitary, there's not much that can touch you."

"I want a TV."

"I'm sure that can be arranged, if you give me something."

"Young. That's the guy who told the Beasts to come here."

"Is he a member?"

"I don't think so, but it's not like I was ever invited to the important stuff. I'm just a small-town dealer, man. The only thing they expect from me is to sell the stuff they give me and to give them the money."

Brandon looked at Maddox. "Do you recognize the name?"

"Not at all, but then, you know me. I do better with animals than with people." He rubbed Brandon's arm. "Do you have what you needed? We could go home."

Brandon turned back to the glass. Bart was still talking—now that he'd started, he seemed not to want to stop—but what he was saying was of no interest to Brandon. Bart was going to jail. He'd probably die there, one way or another.

Of course, that didn't completely take Brandon's fear away, and he knew he'd have nightmares for a while still, but it helped him feel better. He wanted to focus on his relationship with Maddox and finishing school now and put everything else behind him.

He turned to face Maddox. "We can go."

Maddox looked relieved as he led Brandon out of the station, and Brandon was, too. He knew the problem of the Beasts being in town was far from over, and that more people were probably going to die, but he didn't want to think about it. Nathalie was lucky she hadn't been seriously hurt and that Brandon hadn't been either. She'd be fine, and she'd eventually come back to Gillham. Brandon doubted he could ever trust her again, though, and with that, he realized why Maddox had had such a hard time opening up to him.

It wasn't the same, but they'd both been betrayed by people they loved and trusted entirely. Brandon hated it, but he'd realized he second-guessed most people now, even Lee. It was hard to get over that, and he had to force himself to do it.

"What do you want to do now?" Maddox asked. "We can go to the park, or to the theater. Maybe eat dinner in town?"

"I just want to go home." Brandon was drained, even though he hadn't done much today. His emotions were all over the place, though, and he wanted some alone time with Maddox and their furry babies, spread out on the couch and watching bad movies he wouldn't have to focus on. If that also included a make-out session, then Brandon would be all for it, but in the meantime, he wanted a nap.

"I'd like that, you know," Maddox said in a quiet voice. There was a hint of awe in it, as if he couldn't quite believe what Brandon had said.

Brandon smiled. It was easier to forget about Bart and the Beasts when he was with Maddox. "I like it, too. Take me home, Maddox?"

Maddox smiled. "Always."

You may also enjoy the following from eXtasy Books Inc:

Beloved Fangs
Catherine Lievens

Excerpt

Fyfe didn't want to answer the phone. He already knew who it was. The number was saved on his cell phone under Asshat, but unfortunately, he couldn't actually call the man that. He also had to answer because Asshat would kick his ass if he didn't. He'd probably make a point of visiting the coven just to do it.

"Maurice! What can I do for you?" Fyfe said, hoping to shock Asshat with how happy he sounded. Or at least he hoped he sounded happy, as opposed to annoyed and ready to hang up at any second.

"What the fuck do you think you're doing, Fyfe?" Maurice's voice boomed.

Fyfe grimaced. "Answering my phone?"

"Stop playing the idiot. You know what I'm talking about."

Fyfe knew. How could he not? He leaned back in his chair and looked at the ceiling. "He encroached on my territory. He didn't tell me he was in town. He attacked a friend."

"A friend, but not a coven member."

Fyfe sighed. He knew he should have insisted that Percy become a coven member, but Percy had said no, and Fyfe valued their friendship too much to push. "That doesn't mean I shouldn't protect him. Besides, Vlad attacked and bit a human. You know the punishment for that."

Maurice snorted. "Of course I do. I wrote the damn law. You should have called us, though, instead of meting your own justice."

"I couldn't exactly ask him to wait until your guys got here. Come on, Maurice. No one is going to care. Vlad was nuts. He kept another vampire in chains for years. He came after him once he managed to escape. I should have called the conclave, but we both know you guys would have killed him."

Maurice sighed. "Yes, they would have. And I don't care. But not every conclave member feels the way I do. You shouldn't take advantage of the soft spot I have for you."

Fyfe grinned. "Soft spot, huh?" Maybe he should have called Maurice by the nickname he had for him.

"Don't be an asshole."

"Why did you call? Is it only to berate me, or did you have something else to tell me?"

"Some of the conclave members aren't happy, Fyfe. They wanted to make you pay for what happened."

Fyfe snorted. "As if they would have done anything differently."

"Be that as it may. They're the ones questioning your actions right now, not the opposite. And they're in the conclave, so they are the ones with the power. You need to be careful."

"You know that's never been my forte."

"It's not, but you have to toe the line right now before they find a reason to take the coven away from you."

That was Fyfe's worst fear. He might have never wanted or expected to take over the coven, but he had, and they were his to protect. He swallowed and tried to find a way to tell Maurice he'd behave without actually giving in. "I'll protect the coven," was the only thing he could come up with.

Maurice's voice was softer when he answered. "I know. You take your role seriously. I just wanted to warn you."

Since the conclave had the power to get rid of him and put someone else in charge of the coven, Fyfe was glad for the warning. "Thanks."

"And, Fyfe?"

"Yes?"

"I'm not sure of anything, but I think one of the conclave members has someone inside."

It took Fyfe's brain a second to understand what that meant. "You mean in the coven?"

"Yes. I was given a lot of details about what happened with Vlad. Too many details, if you know what I mean. So be careful, and think about cleaning your act up, yeah?"

"Of course." Who could it be? Fyfe had always known not every member was happy with the way he led the coven. He hadn't expected them to. Everyone had their own opinions, including him, and since he was the coven leader, he was the only one making decisions. Some of the elders didn't like that. They probably would have snatched the spot as coven leader if they'd been able to, but Fyfe had been the one who'd killed the old leader, so the coven was legally his, not theirs.

Never theirs, because Fyfe knew what would happen if he allowed that. "I'll keep my eyes open."

"Good. And let me know if you need anything. And I mean anything, Fyfe. We might not see eye to eye all the time, but you're doing a good job as that coven's leader. I want that to continue. It's one less coven I have to worry about."

Fyfe couldn't help but smile. "Ah, so you do love me."

"I wouldn't call it that."

Maurice hung up without adding anything. Fyfe was still

grinning when he hung up, but that didn't last long, not when he heard the yells in the hallway.

He pushed up from his chair and stomped to the door. The coven knew better than to fight, especially where Fyfe could hear them. He didn't care about fighting as long as he didn't find out about it and it wasn't serious. Some people might think vampires were dead and cold, but when it came to emotions and feelings, nothing could be further from the truth. Being immortal meant they had plenty of time to let things steep until they exploded.

Just like it seemed to have happened in the hallway outside his office.

Andrew and Falkner were hitting each other at the top of the stairs. They didn't even notice Fyfe, not until he grabbed Andrew and pulled him back, Falkner's fist hitting his face instead of Andrew's.

The three of them froze.

Fyfe swore and rubbed his cheek. "What the fuck are the two of you doing?" he snapped.

Andrew looked sheepish. "Sorry. It's nothing."

"Nothing? You two were punching each other outside of my office door. You know I don't want anyone fighting in the house."

"We weren't really fighting."

"My face says otherwise."

Falkner winced. "I'm sorry. But we weren't fighting."

Fyfe sighed. He didn't want to have to police his coven members like a father. He wasn't their father, and just the thought made him shudder in horror, especially when he thought about the elder members. Some of them were twice his age. "I don't care what's going on between the two of you, but take it somewhere else."

Falkner nodded so hard, Fyfe wondered if his head might fall off and bounce down the stairs. "We're going."

"You do that." Fyfe watched them leave. He tried to look at them critically and see if they'd only been playing around.

They weren't shying from each other. In fact, they leaned close enough to whisper like children, so Fyfe was pretty sure Andrew had told him the truth. Whatever it was they'd been fighting over, it wasn't serious.

At least this had been an easy problem to solve. Fyfe's conclave problem wouldn't be solved as smoothly, and Fyfe knew he had to get ready for a fight—a real one this time. He sighed and rubbed his face. It didn't actually hurt, although it had when Falkner had punched him. It gave him an excuse to stop working, though, at least for the rest of the night. Dawn would happen in a few hours, so he still had time to go out for a walk. It was his favorite time of the day—when the streets were empty, and no one thought it weird to find him walking around the city. If he stuck to the worst part of the city, it was guaranteed no one would bother him. It wasn't like he wouldn't be safe, even if some bad people were around. He'd make dog kibble out of them and feed them to the nearest werewolf pack.

Fyfe snuck out of the mansion, praying no one would see him. He knew they'd stop him if they did. There was always at least one problem for him to solve with the coven, and he wasn't up for that right now. He wasn't up for dealing with the coven in any way, shape, or form right now.

He took a deep breath, inhaling the night air. He already felt better. The walls weren't closing in around him anymore. Sometimes, he wished he could leave, abandon the coven he'd never meant to lead, and travel like he'd done for so long. He missed it. He missed being alone, not having anyone depending on him.

But he couldn't change it.

ABOUT THE AUTHOR

Catherine lives in Italy, country of good food and hot men. She used to write fantasy as a child, but it was reading her first gay erotic romance novel that made her realize that that was what she really wanted to write.

After graduating from college in English language and translation, she divides her day between writing, reading, taking care of her son and reading some more.

You can find her on Facebook and Twitter or on her website: authorcatherinelievens.wordpress.com

Email: lievens.catherine@gmail.com

Newsletter: http://eepurl.com/c-uvKn

www.ingramcontent.com/pod-product-compliance
Lightning Source LLC
Chambersburg PA
CBHW060624130626
46555CB00002B/655